序 言

這本「中級英語寫作口說測驗」,是專門為參加全民英語能力分級檢定「中級英語檢定測驗」的讀者而編寫。本書的內容,是針對「中級英語檢定測驗」第二階段的複試測驗。

許多人通過了「中級英語檢定測驗」初試,但是,對於即將面臨的複試,心存不安。原因是,在「中級英語檢定測驗」複試中,有口說能力測驗,尤其是問答題的部分,不知如何回答。本書內的問答題,全部經過劉毅英文「中級英檢複試班」,實際在課堂上使用過。該班同學,參加「中級英語檢定複試」後,都高分通過。參加考試的同學都反應,這套試題很有用,和實際考試非常接近。書中朗讀的部分,是由美籍專業錄音員所錄製而成,語調及發音非常純正,讀者可以多練習幾遍。

這本書原來是劉毅英文「中級英檢複試班」的上課講義,第一屆考試,本書幾乎完全命中,考試的作文題目是「寫一封英文信」,在八個不同的考場,總共有八種不同的版本,因此,未來可能還會再考。

口說能力測驗的問答題,本書全部概括,第一次考的是:"What do you like to eat?" "What is your favorite season?" "How did you get here?" "What television program did you watch last night?" 等,這些資料,在書中都有,讀者只要熟讀本書,就可輕易通過複試。如果沒有信心,可參加劉毅英文「中級英檢複試班」。

編者 謹識

本書製作過程

　　本書大部份試題,是由郭昱雯老師命題,石支齊及蔡琇瑩兩位老師負責全部的詳解,並經過美籍老師 Andy Swarzman、Laura E. Stewart,及 Bill Allen 和蔡文華及謝靜芳兩位老師詳細校對。八份試題全部都由劉毅英文「中級英檢複試班」實際在課堂上使用過,報名本班參加複試的同學,錄取率達 87.5 %。

中級英語檢定測驗第二階段

寫作口說能力測驗 ①

寫作能力測驗

一、中譯英（40分）

說明：請將下列的一段中文翻譯成通順、達意且前後連貫的英文。

　　因為使英文成為日常生活中的一部份，是學習英文最好的方式，所以你應該儘可能經常使用它。例如，你可以養成用英文寫日記的習慣來增進寫作能力。藉著每天閱讀英文報紙，你可以增加字彙。在課堂上，找機會發言，並試著用英文和同學溝通。

二、英文作文（60分）

說明：請依下面所提供的文字提示寫一篇英文作文，長度約一百二十字（8至12個句子）。作文可以是一個完整的段落，也可以分段。（評分重點包括內容、組織、文法、用字遣詞、標點符號、大小寫）

提示：很多人都喜歡看電視。請寫一篇文章說明電視如何影響了我們的生活。

口說能力測驗

* 請在 15 秒內完成並唸出下列自我介紹的句子，請開始：

My seat number is __（複試座位號碼後 5 碼）__ , and my registration number is __（初試准考證號碼後 5 碼）__ .

一、朗讀短文

請先利用 1 分鐘的時間閱讀下面的短文，然後在 2 分鐘內以正常的速度，清楚正確的朗讀下面的短文。

An active learner always takes a positive attitude towards his studies. He enjoys using English even if he may make mistakes. He knows making mistakes is natural. In fact, from the mistakes, he learns more. Instead of relying on his teacher for everything, he takes a special interest in learning on his own. With such an attitude, an active learner never quits until he achieves success.

*　　　　*　　　　*

In the world where most people are right-handed, nearly everything was made for right-handed people. However, the left-handed are not forgotten. There are products manufactured to make living easier for left-handed people, such as left-handed scissors, desks, buttons on coats, knives, etc.

According to some doctors, there is a relationship between automobile accidents and suicide. Many accidents happen because the drivers have been drinking. And others occur because the drivers speed or drive recklessly. In fact, these accidents would be avoided if the drivers wanted to. That's why many doctors suggest that such accidents are drivers' self-destructive behaviors.

二、回答問題

這個部分共有 10 題。題目已事先錄音，每題經由耳機播出二次，不印在試題冊上。第 1 至 5 題，每題回答時間 15 秒；第 6 至 10 題，每題回答時間 30 秒。每題播出後，請立即回答。回答時，不一定要用完整的句子，但請在作答時間內儘量的表達。

三、看圖敘述

下面有一張圖片及四個相關的問題,請在 1 分半鐘內完成作答。作答時,請直接回答,不需將題號及題目唸出。首先請利用 30 秒的時間看圖及問題。

1. 你喜歡搭公車嗎?
2. 爲什麼?
3. 圖片中人們在做什麼?
4. 如果還有時間,請詳細敘述圖片中的人、事、物。

*請將下列自我介紹的句子再唸一遍,請開始:

My seat number is ___(複試座位號碼後 5 碼)___, and my registration number is ___(初試准考證號碼後 5 碼)___.

寫作口說能力測驗 ① 詳解

寫作能力測驗詳解

一、中譯英（40分）

因爲使英文成爲日常生活中的一部份，是學習英文最好的方式，所以你應該儘可能經常使用它。例如，你可以養成用英文寫日記的習慣來增進寫作能力。藉著每天閱讀英文報紙，你可以增加字彙。在課堂上，找機會發言，並試著用英文和同學溝通。

Making English part of your daily life is the best way to learn English, so you should use it as often as possible. For example, you can start the habit of keeping a diary in English to improve your writing ability. By reading English newspapers every day, you can increase your vocabulary. In class, take every opportunity to speak out, and try to communicate with your classmates in English.

【註】 diary (ˈdaɪərɪ) *n.* 日記
improve (ɪmˈpruv) *v.* 改善；增進　　***speak out*** 大聲說
communicate (kəˈmjunəˌket) *v.* 溝通
start the habit 養成習慣
= form the habit
= acquire the habit
= get into the habit

二、英文作文（60分）

【作文範例】

　　A fierce debate has been on for years over the pros and cons of television. Whether you believe that its overall effect is positive or negative, everyone agrees that its influence is wide and deep.

　　Television can be entertaining and informative. It allows us to see the world without ever leaving the comfort of our homes. On the other hand, some people believe that the negative impacts of television outweigh its benefits. The biggest complaint is simply that people watch it too much, becoming "couch potatoes." Thus, they may exercise, read, and socialize less. What's worse, watching too much television turns students away from their studies. Furthermore, programs with graphic violence have negative effects on impressionable youths. They often imitate what they've seen on television, leading them to commit serious crimes.

　　Whichever side you take in the great television debate, there's no underestimating the effect television has in today's world.

【註】 fierce〔fɪrs〕adj. 激烈的

debate〔dɪ'bet〕n. 辯論

on〔ɑn〕adv. 繼續；進行（on 在動詞後面，表示「繼續」）

pros and cons 利與弊

overall〔'ovɚˌɔl〕adj. 全面的

effect〔ɪ'fɛkt〕n. 影響

positive〔'pɑzətɪv〕adj. 正面的

negative〔'nɛɡətɪv〕adj. 負面的

influence〔'ɪnfluəns〕n. 影響

entertaining〔ˌɛntɚ'tenɪŋ〕adj. 有趣的

informative〔ɪn'fɔrmətɪv〕adj. 增進知識的；增長見聞的

comfort〔'kʌmfɚt〕n. 舒適

impact〔'ɪmpækt〕n. 影響

outweigh〔aut'we〕v. 勝過　　benefit〔'bɛnəfɪt〕n. 利益

complaint〔kəm'plent〕n. 抱怨

couch potato 整天躺在沙發上看電視的懶人

socialize〔'soʃəˌlaɪz〕v. 交際　　**turn away** 使偏離；避開

studies〔'stʌdɪz〕n. pl. 課業

furthermore〔'fɝðɚˌmor〕adv. 此外

graphic〔'ɡræfɪk〕adj. 生動的；寫實的

violence〔'vaɪələns〕n. 暴力

impressionable〔ɪm'prɛʃənəbl̩〕adj. 易受影響的

youth〔juθ〕n. 年輕人　　imitate〔'ɪməˌtet〕v. 模仿

lead〔lid〕v. 使得　　commit〔kə'mɪt〕v. 犯（罪）

crime〔kraɪm〕n. 罪　　**take~side** 支持~方

there is no + V-ing ~是不可能的（= it is impossible to + V.）

underestimate〔ˌʌndɚ'ɛstəˌmet〕v. 低估

口說能力測驗詳解

＊請在 15 秒內完成並唸出下列自我介紹的句子，請開始：

My seat number is ＿＿＿(複試座位號碼後 5 碼)＿＿＿, and my
registration number is ＿＿(初試准考證號碼後 5 碼)＿＿.

一、朗讀短文

請先利用 1 分鐘的時間閱讀下面的短文，然後在 2 分鐘內以正常的速度，清楚正確的朗讀下面的短文。

An active learner always takes a positive attitude towards his studies. He enjoys using English even if he may make mistakes. He knows making mistakes is natural. In fact, from the mistakes, he learns more. Instead of relying on his teacher for everything, he takes a special interest in learning on his own. With such an attitude, an active learner never quits until he achieves success.

一個主動的學習者，對其學業總是抱持積極的態度。即使可能會犯錯，他仍喜歡使用英文。他知道犯錯是自然的事。事實上，從所犯的錯誤中，他學到更多。他不會凡事都依賴老師，反而對自我學習特別地有興趣。有了這樣的態度，一個主動的學習者，在還未達到成功之前，是不會放棄的。

【註】 active ('æktɪv) adj. 主動的
positive ('pɑzətɪv) adj. 主動的；積極的
attitude ('ætə‚tjud) n. 態度　　**even if** 即使
natural ('nætʃərəl) adj. 自然的　　**instead of** 而不是
rely (rɪ'laɪ) v. 依賴 <on>
take an interest in 對～有興趣　　**on one's own** 靠自己
quit (kwɪt) v. 停止；放棄　　achieve (ə'tʃiv) v. 達到

In the world where most people are right-handed, nearly everything was made for right-handed people. However, the left-handed are not forgotten. There are products manufactured to make living easier for left-handed people, such as left-handed scissors, desks, buttons on coats, knives, etc.

這世界大部份的人，都是右撇子，幾乎所有的東西，都是為他們而設計。然而，左撇子的人可沒被忽略。有些產品是針對左撇子，要讓他們生活更簡便而製造的，例如左手剪刀、書桌、外套鈕扣、刀子等。

【註】 right-handed (ˈraɪtˈhændɪd) adj. 習慣用右手的
　　　nearly (ˈnɪrlɪ) adv. 幾乎
　　　left-handed (ˈlɛftˈhændɪd) adj. 習慣用左手的
　　　product (ˈprɑdəkt , -dʌkt) n. 產品
　　　manufacture (ˌmænjəˈfæktʃɚ) v. 製造
　　　scissors (ˈsɪzɚz) n. pl. 剪刀
　　　button (ˈbʌtn̩) n. 鈕扣　　knife (naɪf) n. 刀子
　　　etc.= et cetera (ɛtˈsɛtərə) 等等

According to some doctors, there is a relationship between automobile accidents and suicide. Many accidents happen because the drivers have been drinking. And others occur because the drivers speed or drive recklessly. In fact, these accidents would be avoided if the drivers wanted to. That's why many doctors suggest that such accidents are drivers' self-destructive behaviors.

根據一些醫生的說法，車禍和自殺是有關係的。許多車禍發生的原因是，駕駛人喝了酒。還有些車禍的發生，是因爲駕駛人超速或開車太魯莽。事實上，如果駕駛人有心避免車禍發生，這些車禍是可以避免的。這就是爲什麼許多醫生表示，這些車禍可說是駕駛人想自殺的行爲。

【註】 relationship〔rɪˋleʃənˏʃɪp〕 *n.* 關係

automobile〔ˏɔtəˋmobɪl〕 *n.* 汽車

accident〔ˋæksədənt〕 *n.* 意外；車禍

suicide〔ˋsuəˏsaɪd〕 *n.* 自殺　　speed〔spid〕 *v.* 超速行駛

recklessly〔ˋrɛklɪslɪ〕 *adv.* 魯莽地

avoid〔əˋvɔɪd〕 *v.* 避免

self-destructive〔ˏsɛlfdɪˋstrʌktɪv〕 *adj.* 自我毀滅的；自殺的

behavior〔bɪˋhevjɚ〕 *n.* 行爲

二、回答問題

這個部分共有 10 題。題目已事先錄音，每題經由耳機播出二次，不印在試題冊上。第 1 至 5 題，每題回答時間 15 秒；第 6 至 10 題，每題回答時間 30 秒。每題播出後，請立即回答。回答時，不一定要用完整的句子，但請在作答時間內儘量的表達。

※ 第 1 至第 5 題，每題回答時間 15 秒。

1. Q ： Are you nervous now? If yes, why, if no, why not?

你現在會緊張嗎？如果會，爲什麼？如果不會，爲什麼？

A1： Yes. I am a little nervous, because I have never been through this type of test before.

是的，我有點緊張，因爲我以前從沒參加過這類型的測驗。

A2： No. I am not nervous, because I am very confident of my English ability.

不，我不緊張，因為我對我的英文能力非常有信心。

2. Q ： What do you love to do on weekends?

週末你喜歡做什麼？

A1： I love to go shopping.

我喜歡逛街。

A2： I love to go to the movies on weekends.

我喜歡在週末去看電影。

A3： I love to go hiking.　我喜歡健行。

3. Q ： What is your favorite subject?　Why?

你最喜歡什麼科目？為什麼？

A1： English.　Because my teacher makes it interesting for me to learn.

英文。因為我的老師讓學習英文變得很有趣。

A2： Math.　I find math a very interesting subject.

數學。我覺得數學是很有趣的科目。

A3： History.　I was able to learn a lot about what had happened before and why it happened.

歷史。我可以學到很多從前發生的事，及其發生的原因。

【註】　1. nervous (ˈnɝvəs) adj. 緊張的
confident (ˈkɑnfədənt) adj. 有信心的
ability (əˈbɪlətɪ) n. 能力
2. hiking (ˈhaɪkɪŋ) n. 健行

4. Q ： How do you like fast food restaurants?

你覺得速食店如何？

A1 ： I like going to fast food restaurants. The food is good and the price is affordable.

我喜歡去速食店，食物不錯，價格也是我負擔得起的。

A2 ： I don't like fast food, because I don't think it is healthy. So I don't really go to fast food restaurants.

我不喜歡速食，因為我覺得那是不健康的。所以其實我不會去速食店。

---

5. Q ： What would you do if an earthquake occurred now?

如果現在發生地震，你會怎麼辦？

A1 ： I would panic. 我會很恐慌。

A2 ： I would hide under the doorframe.

我會躲在門框下。

A3 ： I would try to get to an open area as quickly as I could.

我會儘快跑到空地上。

※ 第 6 至第 10 題，每題回答時間 30 秒。

6. Q ： Tell me about the most impressive movie you have ever seen. Why were you impressed by it?

談談你所看過印象最深刻的電影，以及為什麼？

【註】 4. affordable 〔 ə'fɔrdəbḷ 〕 *adj.* 負擔得起的

5. panic 〔'pænɪk 〕 *v.* 感到恐慌

earthquake 〔'ɝθ,kwek 〕 *n.* 地震

doorframe 〔'dor,frem 〕 *n.* 門框　　***open area*** 空地

6. impressive 〔 ɪm'prɛsɪv 〕 *adj.* 令人印象深刻的

A1 : It would be "The Titanic." The story was a real
tear-jerker.

應該是「鐵達尼號」。那個故事眞是太悲慘了。

A2 : "The Legend of the Sacred Stone." This movie
promotes traditional Taiwanese folk art and it also
has great special effects.

「聖石傳說」。這部電影提倡了台灣的傳統民俗藝術，而且
特效做得很棒。

7. Q : Which do you think is a better means of communication,
calling somebody by phone or writing a letter? Why?

你覺得哪一種聯絡方式比較好，打電話還是寫信？爲什麼？

A1 : Calling somebody by phone is better, because we can
hear the person who we are talking to. It is also a lot
faster than writing letters.

打電話比較好，因爲這樣可以聽到對方的聲音，而且也比
寫信快多了。

A2 : Writing letters is better than calling someone on the
phone. It is cheaper to write somebody a letter,
especially when the recipient is overseas.

寫信比打電話好。寫信比較省錢，尤其是對方在國外的時候。

【註】　6. tear-jerker ('tɪr,dʒɝkɚ) n. 主題悲慘之電影
legend ('lɛdʒənd) n. 傳奇　　sacred ('sekrɪd) adj. 神聖的
promote (prə'mot) v. 提倡　　*folk art* 民俗藝術

7. means (minz) n. pl. 方法
communication (kə,mjunə'keʃən) n. 連絡
recipient (rɪ'sɪpənt) n. 接受者；受話者
overseas ('ovɚ'siz) adj. 在國外的

8. Q : When you feel sad or depressed, what do you do to cheer yourself up?

　　　當你難過或沮喪時，你會如何使自己振作起來？

A1 : Whenever I am sad, I will go to a KTV and sing. By doing so, I can forget about my sadness.

　　　每當我覺得難過時，我會去 KTV 唱歌。這樣可以讓我忘記悲傷。

A2 : When I am depressed, I will talk to my friends and tell them about my problems.

　　　當我沮喪時，我會和朋友聊聊，把問題告訴他們。

A3 : I will try not to think about it and I'll be happy again.　我會試著不去想它，然後我就會快樂起來。

---

9. Q : Do you think Taipei is a good place to live? State the reasons for your answer.

　　　你覺得台北適合居住嗎？請說出你的理由。

A1 : Of course, it is.　Taipei has everything I could ever need and it is convenient for people to go places with the MRT system in operation.

　　　當然是。我需要的東西台北都有，而且因為有捷運，所以到哪裏都很方便。

【註】　8. depressed (dɪˈprɛst) adj. 沮喪的
　　　　　　cheer up 使高興；使振作
　　　　　9. state (stet) v. 說明
　　　　　　MRT 捷運 (= *Mass Rapid Transit*)
　　　　　　in operation 運作中

A2：No, I don't think Taipei is a good place to live.　Taipei is too crowded and the traffic situation is terrible.

　　不，我不認爲台北是個適合居住的地方。台北太擁擠了，而且交通狀況也很糟。

A3：No. Because it rains all the time.　不適合。因爲台北常下雨。

~~~~~~~~~~~~~~~~~~~~~~~~~~

10. Q ：Would you rather study in a coed school or a girls' school or a boys' school?

　　你比較喜歡在男女合校，還是男女分校讀書？

A1：I would like to be in a coed school; that way I can meet friends of the opposite sex.

　　我喜歡男女合校，這樣我就可以認識異性朋友。

A2：I would rather be in a boys' school.

　　我喜歡男女分校。

【註】 9. crowded〔ˈkraʊdɪd〕*adj.* 擁擠的

三、看圖敘述

下面有一張圖片及四個相關的問題，請在 1 分半鐘內完成作答。作答時，請直接回答，不需將題號及題目唸出。首先請利用 30 秒的時間看圖及問題。

1. 你喜歡搭公車嗎？爲什麼？

No, I don't like to take the bus.

　　不，我不喜歡搭公車。

2. 爲什麼？

It takes too long and the bus is often crowded.

　　搭公車太花時間了，而且公車上經常很擁擠。

3. 圖片中人們在做什麼？

   It looks like they are taking the bus.

   他們看起來像是在搭公車。

4. 如果還有時間，請詳細敘述圖片中的人、事、物。

   These people are on a bus, either going to work or school. There are two female students standing in the middle of the bus, and one of them is studying. A man in the bottom left corner of the picture wants to smoke a cigarette, and the man sitting next to him is using a calculator. On the bottom right of the picture is a man who seems to be pressed for time. The other people on the bus are either dozing or talking.

   公車上的這些人，不是去上班，就是去上學。在公車的中央，站著兩位女學生，其中的一個在唸書。圖片左下角的男人想要抽菸，坐在他旁邊的男人在使用計算機。圖片右下角的男人似乎在趕時間。公車上其他的人不是在打瞌睡，就是在聊天。

   【註】 4. calculator ('kælkjə,letə) n. 計算機
           be pressed for time 趕時間
           doze (doz) v. 打瞌睡

* 請將下列自我介紹的句子再唸一遍，請開始：

   My seat number is ___（複試座位號碼後 5 碼）___, and my registration number is ___（初試准考證號碼後 5 碼）___.

GEPT® 全民英語能力分級檢定測驗
中級寫作能力測驗答案紙

座位號碼：_____   試卷別：_____

第一部分請由第1行開始作答，請勿隔行書寫。

_____

_____

_____

_____

_____

_____

_____

_____

_____

_____

_____

_____

_____

_____

_____

_____

_____

_____

_____

第二部分請翻至第2頁作答

25

30

35

40

中級英語檢定測驗第二階段

寫作口說能力測驗②

寫作能力測驗

一、中譯英（40 分）

說明：請將下列的一段中文翻譯成通順、達意且前後連貫的英文。

　　瑪麗在她 30 歲的生日上說：「我希望我今年能到歐洲去旅行。」但她是不可能實現這個願望的。原因是她既沒時間也沒有錢去旅行。自她丈夫被解雇後，她們家就得凡事將就，更遑論要花錢去歐洲旅行了。此外，她還有三個小孩要照顧呢。但無論我怎麼勸她放棄這個計劃，她仍不放棄這個夢想。

二、英文作文（60 分）

說明：請依下面所提供的文字提示寫一篇英文作文，長度約一百二十字（8 至 12 個句子）。作文可以是一個完整的段落，也可以分段。（評分重點包括內容、組織、文法、用字遣詞、標點符號、大小寫）

提示：你曾經仔細的看過日出和日落嗎？你喜歡嗎？請寫一篇文章表達你對日出和日落的感想。

口説能力測驗

* 請在 15 秒內完成並唸出下列自我介紹的句子，請開始：

My seat number is ___(複試座位號碼後5碼)___, and my
registration number is ___(初試准考證號碼後5碼)___.

一、朗讀短文

請先利用 1 分鐘的時間閱讀下面的短文，然後在 2 分鐘內以正常的
速度，清楚正確的朗讀下面的短文。

Mercury is one of the strangest of all metals
because it is a liquid at regular temperatures. It is
used in thermometers and barometers. The silvery
liquid was what suggested the name "quicksilver"
for mercury. When poured out, it forms into tiny
balls that are hard to pick up.

         *   *   *

A 10-year-old Russian girl is preparing to have a
heart surgery. Doctors in Russia will freeze the girl
to the point of death, which is believed to protect her
from brain damage. The doctors use the technique
by cooling the body with ice to temperatures of 23 °C
to 25 °C. This technique can decrease the rate of
metabolism, reducing the body's need for oxygen.

There is physical evidence that UFOs have been present in a given location. This evidence includes markings on the ground and fragments of debris discharged from the UFOs. In many cases the debris is confiscated by government personnel. However, some evidence of UFOs has slipped out of the government's hands.

二、回答問題

這個部分共有 10 題。題目已事先錄音，每題經由耳機播出二次，不印在試題冊上。第 1 至 5 題，每題回答時間 15 秒；第 6 至 10 題，每題回答時間 30 秒。每題播出後，請立即回答。回答時，不一定要用完整的句子，但請在作答時間內儘量的表達。

三、看圖敘述

下面有一張圖片及三個相關的問題，請在 1 分半鐘內完成作答。作答時，請直接回答，不需將題號及題目唸出。首先請利用 30 秒的時間看圖及問題。

1. 這裡是什麼地方？
2. 照片裡的人在做什麼？
3. 請對圖中的人、事、物做敘述。

*請將下列自我介紹的句子再唸一遍，請開始：

My seat number is ___(複試座位號碼後 5 碼)___ , and my registration number is ___(初試准考證號碼後 5 碼)___ .

寫作口説能力測驗 ② 詳解

寫作能力測驗詳解

一、中譯英（40分）

　　瑪麗在她30歲的生日上說：「我希望我今年能到歐洲去旅行。」但她是不可能實現這個願望的。原因是她既沒時間也沒有錢去旅行。自她丈夫被解雇後，他們家就得凡事將就，更遑論要花錢去歐洲旅行了。此外，她還有三個小孩要照顧呢。但無論我怎麼勸她放棄這個計劃，她仍不放棄這個夢想。

"I wish I could travel to Europe this year," Mary said on her thirtieth birthday. But it is impossible for her wish to come true. The reason is that she has neither time nor money to go traveling. Ever since her husband was laid off, her family has had to make do with what they have, let alone to spend money on a trip to Europe. In addition, she has three children to care for. But no matter how hard I try to talk her out of this plan, she will not give up this dream.

【註】 *come true* 實現　　*neither* A *nor* B 既不是 A 也不是 B
lay off 解雇　　*make do* 將就使用
let alone 更不用說　　*in addition* 此外
care for 照顧　　*talk sb. out of* 勸某人放棄～
give up 放棄

二、英文作文（60分）

【作文範例】

　　In my opinion, the most beautiful times of the day are sunrise and sunset. They are not only colorful, but are usually quiet and peaceful. Watching the sun rise and set gives me a chance to think about life.

　　I often watch the sunrise. When I see the sky light up, I know a new day is beginning. I feel as if the world has come back to life. This quiet time enables me to think about the day ahead of me. Furthermore, the beautiful scene inspires me to do my best, and to study hard. As the sun rises higher and becomes brighter, I can feel the strength of its energy.

　　The sunset gives me a very different feeling, though. It is sometimes even more beautiful than the sunrise. It makes me think about my life and my future. Our lives are short, and eventually we all must die. Accordingly, we should use our time well. We should also cherish what we have. This is what I learn from watching the sunset.

【註】 opinion〔ə'pɪnjən〕n. 意見

sunrise〔'sʌn,raɪz〕n. 日出

not only…**but**（**also**）~　不只…還~

sunset〔'sʌn,sɛt〕n. 日落　　quiet〔'kwaɪət〕adj. 安靜的

peaceful〔'pisfəl〕adj. 詳和的

chance〔tʃæns〕n. 機會　　**light up** 變亮

come（**back**）**to life** 甦醒　　enable〔ɪn'ebl〕v. 使能夠

furthermore〔'fɝðɚ,mor〕adv. 此外

scene〔sin〕n. 景色　　inspire〔ɪn'spaɪr〕v. 激勵

do one's **best** 盡力　　hard〔hɑrd〕adv. 認眞地

strength〔strɛŋθ〕n. 力量　　energy〔'ɛnɚdʒɪ〕n. 活力

though〔ðo〕adv. 可是　　future〔'fjutʃɚ〕n. 未來

eventually〔ɪ'vɛntʃʊəlɪ〕adv. 到最後

accordingly〔ə'kɔrdɪŋlɪ〕adv. 因此

cherish〔'tʃɛrɪʃ〕v. 珍惜

　　英文作文得高分的祕訣是，字要寫得整齊，字數要多，必須超過 120 字以上，愈多愈好，不能有塗改。在考試時，要記得攜帶 2B 鉛筆。目前只有此項考試是用鉛筆寫作文。

口說能力測驗詳解

* 請在 15 秒內完成並唸出下列自我介紹的句子，請開始：

My seat number is ___(複試座位號碼後 5 碼)___, and my
registration number is ___(初試准考證號碼後 5 碼)___.

一、朗讀短文

請先利用 1 分鐘的時間閱讀下面的短文，然後在 2 分鐘內以正常的速度，清楚正確的朗讀下面的短文。

Mercury is one of the strangest of all metals because it is a liquid at regular temperatures. It is used in thermometers and barometers. The silvery liquid was what suggested the name "quicksilver" for mercury. When poured out, it forms into tiny balls that are hard to pick up.

水銀是所有金屬中，最奇特的金屬之一，因為它在常溫下是液體。它被用於溫度計和氣壓計當中。這銀色的液體，使人想要把水銀命名為「快速流動的銀」。當水銀被倒出來，它會形成一顆顆小小的球狀物，很難拿起來。

【註】 mercury ('mɝkjərɪ) *n.* 水銀；汞　　metal ('mɛtḷ) *n.* 金屬
liquid ('lɪkwɪd) *n.* 液體
regular ('rɛgjələ) *adj.* 正常的；一般的
temperature ('tɛmprətʃə) *n.* 溫度
thermometer (θə'mamətə) *n.* 溫度計
barometer (bə'ramətə) *n.* 氣壓計
silvery ('sɪlvərɪ) *adj.* 銀色的
suggest (sə'dʒɛst) *v.* 使聯想到　　pour (por) *v.* 倒出
form (fɔrm) *v.* 形成　　tiny ('taɪnɪ) *adj.* 微小的

A 10-year-old Russian girl is preparing to have a heart surgery. Doctors in Russia will freeze the girl to the point of death, which is believed to protect her from brain damage. The doctors use the technique by cooling the body with ice to temperatures of 23 °C to 25 °C. This technique can decrease the rate of metabolism, reducing the body's need for oxygen.

有位十歲的俄國女孩，正準備進行心臟手術。俄國的醫生會將她冷凍到接近死亡的程度，一般認為，這樣的方式可保護她的腦部，避免受到傷害。醫生採用這種技術，用冰使其體溫降到攝氏 23 度至 25 度。這項技術可降低新陳代謝的速度，以減少身體對氧氣的需求。

【註】 Russian〔ˈrʌʃən〕adj. 俄國的
　　　 surgery〔ˈsɝdʒərɪ〕n. 外科手術
　　　 freeze〔friz〕v. 冷凍　　point〔pɔɪnt〕n. 程度
　　　 protect〔prəˈtɛkt〕v. 保護　　brain〔bren〕n. 腦
　　　 damage〔ˈdæmɪdʒ〕n. 傷害　　technique〔tɛkˈnik〕n. 技術
　　　 cool〔kul〕v. 使冷卻　　rate〔ret〕n. 速度
　　　 metabolism〔mɛˈtæbḷɪzəm〕n. 新陳代謝
　　　 reduce〔rɪˈdjus〕v. 減少　　oxygen〔ˈɑksədʒən〕n. 氧

There is physical evidence that UFOs have been present in a given location. This evidence includes markings on the ground and fragments of debris discharged from the UFOs. In many cases the debris is confiscated by government personnel. However, some evidence of UFOs has slipped out of the government's hands.

　　有具體的證據顯示，不明飛行物體曾在一特定地點出現過。
證據包括留在地上的痕跡，以及不明飛行物體留下的殘骸碎片。
通常這些殘骸會被政府人員沒收。然而，有些關於不明飛行物體
的證據，已從政府的手中洩露出來。

【註】 ***UFO*** 不明飛行物體 (= *Unidentified Flying Object*)
　　　 physical (ˈfɪzɪkḷ) *adj.* 具體的　　evidence (ˈɛvədəns) *n.* 證據
　　　 present (ˈprɛzn̩t) *adj.* 存在的　　 given (ˈgɪvən) *adj.* 特定的
　　　 location (loˈkeʃən) *n.* 地點　　　marking (ˈmarkɪŋ) *n.* 痕跡
　　　 fragment (ˈfrægmənt) *n.* 碎片
　　　 debris (dəˈbri , ˈdebri) *n.* 殘骸
　　　 discharge (dɪsˈtʃardʒ) *v.* 排出；卸下
　　　 confiscate (ˈkɑnfɪsˌket) *v.* 沒收
　　　 government (ˈgʌvənmənt) *n.* 政府
　　　 personnel (ˌpɝsn̩ˈɛl) *n.* 人員
　　　 slip (slɪp) *v.* 在無意中講出；被洩漏

二、回答問題

這個部分共有 10 題。題目已事先錄音，每題經由耳機播出二次，不印
在試題冊上。第 1 至 5 題，每題回答時間 15 秒；第 6 至 10 題，每題回
答時間 30 秒。每題播出後，請立即回答。回答時，不一定要用完整的
句子，但請在作答時間內儘量的表達。

※ 第 1 至第 5 題，每題回答時間 15 秒。

1. Q ： What are you doing now? 你現在在做什麼？

　　A1 ： I am taking the oral test for the Intermediate English
　　　　　 Proficiency Test.
　　　　　 我正在參加中級英語檢定口試。

　　【註】 1. oral (ˈɔrəl) *adj.* 口頭的

A2：I am taking a test.　I hope that I can pass this test.

　　我正在考試。我希望我能通過這項測驗。

---

2. Q　：What will you do after the test?

　　考完試後你要做什麼？

A1：I will go shopping with my friends after the test.

　　考完試後我要和我的朋友去購物。

A2：I will go home and sleep, because I woke up early this morning to prepare for this test.

　　我要回家去睡覺，因為我今天早上很早起床準備這個考試。

A3：I will go see a movie.　I had spent a lot of time studying and I need to take a break.

　　我要去看電影。我花了許多時間唸書，所以我需要休息一下。

---

3. Q　：When you catch a cold, what should you do to help yourself recover quickly?

　　當你感冒的時候，你應該怎麼做才能幫助自己早日康復？

A1：I believe that taking a lot of vitamin C will help me recover sooner.

　　我認為服用大量的維他命 C，將有助於我早日康復。

【註】　2. *take a break* 休息一下（ = *take a rest* ）

　　　　3. recover〔rɪˋkʌvɚ〕*v.* 恢復

　　　　plenty of 很多的

A2 : I will take a long hot bath followed by a long nap. Getting plenty of rest always helps me recover from my illness.

我會好好地洗個熱水澡，然後再好好地睡一覺。多休息一定有助於我早日康復。

A3 : I will eat a lot of fruit and rest a lot.

我會吃很多水果並多休息。

A4 : I will not do anything. I believe that if I get sick, I should just suck it up and let nature take its course.

我不會做任何事。我認為如果我生病的話，就應該忍一下，讓它自然而然地痊癒。

---

4. Q : Here is a situation: You are on your way home, but suddenly, it begins to rain. Unfortunately, you have no umbrella with you. What will you do?

現在這裡有一個狀況：你正在回家的路上，可是突然間下起雨來。很不幸地，你沒帶雨傘。你會怎麼做？

A1 : If I get caught in the rain without an umbrella, I will find the nearest store which sells umbrellas and buy one.

如果我遇到下雨卻沒有帶傘，我會找一家最近的，有賣傘的商店，買一把傘。

A2 : I will take a taxi to where I want to go.

我會搭計程車到我想去的地方。

【註】 3. *suck it up* 忍受住
　　　　let nature take its course 順其自然
　　　4. *get caught in* 遇到（雨）

A3 : I will go shopping until the rain stops.

我會去購物，直到雨停爲止。

A4 : I really don't care about the rain. I will not let a few drops of water stop me from doing what I have to do, even if it means that I will have to get wet.

我不太在意下雨。我不會讓幾滴水，阻擋我去做我必須做的事，即使這意謂著我必須淋溼。

---

5. Q : Which do you like better, city life or country life?

你比較喜歡哪一種生活，是都市生活還是鄉村生活？

A1 : I think I would prefer country life. I am so sick and tired of the noisy and crowded city. Sometimes seeing nothing but cars, people, and high-rise buildings drives me up the wall.

我想我比較喜歡鄉村生活。我對吵鬧、擁擠的都市，感到非常厭倦。除了汽車、人群，和高樓大廈以外，什麼都看不到，有時候這樣會把我逼瘋。

A2 : I am a city person. I can not bear the thought of living in the country where nothing is convenient. I enjoy the excitement and convenience that city life offers.

我是個都市人。我無法想像生活在凡事都不方便的鄉下。我很喜歡都市生活所提供的刺激與便利。

【註】 5. *drive sb.* ***up the wall*** 把某人逼瘋

※ 第 6 至第 10 題，每題回答時間 30 秒。

6. Q : What kind of music do you like most? Why?

　　　你最喜歡哪一種音樂？爲什麼？

　　A1 : I like to listen to country western. Because I enjoy listening to the stories they tell. The beautiful melodies also connect me with mankind.

　　　　我喜歡聽西部鄉村音樂，因爲我喜歡聽歌詞裡所說的故事。它優美的旋律使我和人類有所交流。

　　A2 : I like listening to Japanese popular music. It is the fashionable thing to do. If I don't keep up with the latest trend, I would be the laughingstock of my school.

　　　　我喜歡聽日本流行音樂，這是一種流行。如果我跟不上最新的時尚，我會成爲學校的笑柄。

　　A3 : I only listen to classic rock. Back then, the music actually meant something. Unlike modern music, which is mostly synthesized, classic rock has more life to it.

　　　　我只聽經典搖滾樂。以前的音樂，眞的有內涵。不像現代的音樂，大多是合成的，經典搖滾樂比較有生命力。

【註】 6. bear (bɛr) v. 忍受　　melody ('mɛlədɪ) n. 旋律
　　　　　connect (kə'nɛkt) v. 溝通
　　　　　trend (trɛnd) n. 時尚
　　　　　laughingstock ('læfɪŋ,stɑk) n. 笑柄
　　　　　classic ('klæsɪk) adj. 經典的
　　　　　synthesize ('sɪnθə,saɪz) v. 合成

7. Q ：Do you like traveling?　Why?

　　　你喜歡旅行嗎？爲什麼？

A1：No.　I am really uncomfortable in a place I am not familiar with.　I also don't like to go places where I don't speak the language.

　　　不喜歡。待在一個陌生的地方，會讓我感到很不舒服。我也不喜歡去我語言不通的地方。

A2：I love to go traveling.　There's nothing that I'd rather do.　I love to visit exotic foreign countries and meet exciting people.

　　　我喜歡旅行，勝過做其他事情。我熱愛拜訪充滿異國風情的國家，和遇見令人興奮的人。

---

8. Q ："Money is not everything."　What do you think?

　　　「金錢不是萬能的。」對於這句話，你有什麼看法？

A1：Of course money is everything.　If you don't have money, then you can't have the things you want.

　　　錢當然是萬能的。如果你沒錢，你就不能擁有你想要的東西。

A2：Money is not the only thing, but it certainly is important.　It may not buy a lot of abstract things but it can definitely fulfill your material needs.

　　　錢不是唯一，但它確實很重要。它也許不能買許多抽象的事物，但它一定能滿足你物質上的需要。

【註】　7. exotic〔ɪg'zɑtɪk〕adj. 有異國風味的

　　　　8. abstract〔'æbstrækt〕adj. 抽象的
　　　　　definitely〔'dɛfənɪtlɪ〕adv. 一定地；當然
　　　　　fulfill〔fʊl'fɪl〕v. 滿足
　　　　　material〔mə'tɪrɪəl〕adj. 物質的

9. Q : Describe your mother. 描述一下你的母親。

A1 : My mother is the most wonderful woman. She is a kind-hearted person, full of tenderness and compassion.

我母親是最棒的女人。她是個仁慈、溫柔，而且富有同情心的人。

A2 : My mother is a great woman. She is an excellent teacher and a wonderful parent. She taught me a lot of things, which really influenced me a lot.

我母親是個偉大的女人。她是位優秀的老師，也是個很棒的母親。她教了我許多事情，對我的影響相當大。

---

10. Q : What do you think is the best way to learn English? 你認為學英語最好的方法是什麼？

A1 : The best way to learn English is known as the "total immersion" method. You should get yourself to an English-speaking environment. Expose yourself to as much English as possible.

學英文最好的方法是所謂的「完全沈浸」法。你應該讓自己處於一個說英語的環境。儘量讓自己多接觸英語。

【註】 9. tenderness ('tɛndənɪs) n. 溫柔
compassion (kəm'pæʃən) n. 同情
influence ('ɪnfluəns) v. 影響

10. immersion (ɪ'mɜʃən) n. 沉浸

A2：The best way to learn English is to try not using your mother tongue as much as possible. Practice reading, writing, listening, and speaking all the time. Most important of all, don't be afraid of making mistakes.

學英文最好的方法，是儘量不要使用自己的母語。要不斷地練習聽、說、讀、寫。最重要的是，不要怕犯錯。

【註】　10. expose〔ɪk'spoz〕*v.* 使接觸
mother tongue 母語

三、看圖敘述

下面有一張圖片及三個相關的問題，請在 1 分半鐘內完成作答。作答時，請直接回答，不需將題號及題目唸出。首先請利用 30 秒的時間看圖及問題。

1. 這裡是什麼地方？

This place looks like a classroom at a school.

這個地方看起來像學校的教室。

2. 照片裡的人在做什麼？

These people are having a class. The older gentleman, who appears to be a teacher, is giving a lecture. The young lady is standing by the blackboard listening to the man.

這些人在上課。比較年長的那位先生，看起來像是老師，他正在教課。那位年輕的小姐，正站在黑板旁邊聽他講話。

【註】　2. lecture〔'lɛktʃɚ〕*n.* 講課
blackboard〔'blæk,bord〕*n.* 黑板

3. 請對圖中的人、事、物做敘述。

  This is a classroom. There is a blackboard on the wall. To the right of the blackboard is a bulletin board. There is a table in front of the blackboard. On the table is a school bag and some books. The older man, who is the teacher, is teaching the students. A female student is standing in front of the blackboard, probably just got done writing something on the board and is listening to what the teacher is saying. A sign above the blackboard says that you can't drink or eat in the classroom.

  這是一間教室。牆上有一個黑板。在黑板的右邊是個佈告欄。在黑板的前面有一張桌子。桌上有個書包和一些書本。比較年長的那位先生,是個老師,他正在教學生。有位可能剛剛在黑板上寫完東西的女學生,正站在黑板前面,聽老師講話。在黑板的上方有個牌子,上面寫著,禁止在教室裡飲食。

  【註】 3. bulletin ('bulətɪn) *n.* 佈告
    bulletin board 佈告欄

＊請將下列自我介紹的句子再唸一遍,請開始:

My seat number is ___(複試座位號碼後 5 碼)___ , and my registration number is ___(初試准考證號碼後 5 碼)___ .

GEPT® 全民英語能力分級檢定測驗
中級寫作能力測驗答案紙

座位號碼：＿＿＿＿＿＿＿＿＿＿＿＿　　　試卷別：＿＿＿＿＿＿＿

第一部分請由第1行開始作答，請勿隔行書寫。

25

30

35

40

中級英語檢定測驗第二階段

寫作口說能力測驗 ③

寫作能力測驗

一、中譯英（40分）

說明：請將下列的一段中文翻譯成通順、達意且前後連貫的英文。

　　自從我成為高中生後，我就一直對中國古典小說有興趣。這些書是祖先智慧的結晶；因此，它們值得仔細閱讀。但準備大學聯考使我無法這麼做。我希望當我進入大學後，會有空閒時間全心投入閱讀。

二、英文作文（60分）

說明：請依下面所提供的文字提示寫一篇英文作文，長度約一百二十字（8至12個句子）。作文可以是一個完整的段落，也可以分段。（評分重點包括內容、組織、文法、用字遣詞、標點符號、大小寫）

提示：老師在每個人的求學當中，扮演了非常重要的角色。請寫一篇文章

　　（1）說明你認為一位好老師須具備的條件；

　　（2）形容一位你最喜歡的老師。

口說能力測驗

* 請在 15 秒內完成並唸出下列自我介紹的句子，請開始：

My seat number is ___(複試座位號碼後 5 碼)___, and my
registration number is ___(初試准考證號碼後 5 碼)___.

一、朗讀短文

請先利用 1 分鐘的時間閱讀下面的短文，然後在 2 分鐘內以正常的
速度，清楚正確的朗讀下面的短文。

Bats perform an important ecological function throughout the world. They eat millions of harmful insects yearly. In fact, the food a bat eats every night amounts to one quarter of its own body weight. Scientists have observed a single colony of Arizona bats eat up to 35,000 pounds of insects every night. That's the equivalent weight of 34 elephants.

    *   *   *

We have an adopted daughter whom we love dearly. We also have a biological child. To us there is absolutely no difference between them and of course we wish our adopted daughter felt that way, too. We strongly believe if we can steer her through this emotionally stormy period of adolescence, she will not give another thought to finding her own mother.

The most effective way to help a manufacturer sell more of his products is advertising. Nowadays there are countless advertising agencies, which deal with all the publicity that will promote the sale of goods. Advertisements are found on TV, in newspapers and magazines. In return, the manufacturer has to pay the agency for their services. And it is indeed a large amount of money.

二、回答問題

這個部分共有 10 題。題目已事先錄音，每題經由耳機播出二次，不印在試題冊上。第 1 至 5 題，每題回答時間 15 秒；第 6 至 10 題，每題回答時間 30 秒。每題播出後，請立即回答。回答時，不一定要用完整的句子，但請在作答時間內儘量的表達。

三、看圖敘述

下面有一張圖片及五個相關的問題,請在 1 分半鐘內完成作答。作答時,請直接回答,不需將題號及題目唸出。首先請利用 30 秒的時間看圖及問題。

1. 這是什麼地方?
2. 圖片中的人在做什麼?
3. 你喜歡去海邊嗎?
4. 為什麼?
5. 請詳細敘述圖片中的人、事、物。

*請將下列自我介紹的句子再唸一遍,請開始:

My seat number is ___(複試座位號碼後 5 碼)___, and my registration number is ___(初試准考證號碼後 5 碼)___.

寫作口說能力測驗 ③ 詳解

寫作能力測驗詳解

一、中譯英（40分）

　　自從我成為高中生後，我就一直對中國古典小說有興趣。這些書是祖先智慧的結晶；因此，它們值得仔細閱讀。但準備大學聯考使我無法這麼做。我希望當我進入大學後，會有空閒時間全心投入閱讀。

　　Ever since I became a senior high school student, I have been interested in reading classical Chinese literature. These books are the results of our ancestors' wisdom; therefore, they are worth reading in detail. However, I am not able to do that because I have to prepare for the JCEE. I hope that after I enter college, I will have free time so I can focus on reading.

【註】 ***ever since*** 自從　　classical（ˈklæsɪkḷ）*adj.* 古典的
　　　　literature（ˈlɪtərətʃɚ）*n.* 文學
　　　　result（rɪˈzʌlt）*n.* 成果　　ancestor（ˈænsɛstɚ）*n.* 祖先
　　　　wisdom（ˈwɪzdəm）*n.* 智慧
　　　　be worth + V-ing 值得～　　***in detail*** 詳細地
　　　　JCEE 大學聯考（= *Joint College Entrance Exam*）
　　　　focus（ˈfokəs）*v.* 集中　　***focus on*** 專注於

二、英文作文（60分）

【作文範例】

　　A good teacher is many things to many people. He not only teaches students knowledge from books, but also shares his experiences in life with them. In addition, he also plays the role of a counselor, helping students solve their problems in life. Therefore, we can say that a good teacher has a great influence on his students in every aspect of life.

　　I miss one teacher in particular. She was my Chinese teacher in junior high school. She wore her hair long and had a very even temperament. However, the latter quality was not why students loved her. The reason lay in her concern for them. Though she was very strict about our studies, she was very kind and reliable as a friend. We always shared our secrets with her. She also helped us solve all kinds of problems. If we were sick at school, she was always the first to take us to the doctor. Hence, even students who graduated years ago still keep in touch with her. We still enjoy sharing our happiness and sorrow with her. She'll always be our friend.

【註】 *be many things* 具有許多特性

not only…but (also)~ 不只…還~

knowledge (ˈnɑlɪdʒ) *n.* 知識

experience (ɪkˈspɪrɪəns) *n.* 經驗

in addition 此外　　play (ple) *v.* 扮演

role (rol) *n.* 角色　　share (ʃɛr) *v.* 分享

counselor (ˈkaʊnslə) *n.* 輔導老師

influence (ˈɪnflʊəns) *n.* 影響

aspect (ˈæspɛkt) *n.* 方面　　*in particular* 特別地

wear one's hair long 留長髮

even (ˈivən) *adj.* 沉靜的

temperament (ˈtɛmprəmənt) *n.* 性情

latter (ˈlætə) *adj.* 後者的　　quality (ˈkwɑlətɪ) *n.* 特質

reason (ˈrizn̩) *n.* 原因；理由

lie in 在於　　concern (kənˈsɜn) *n.* 關心

strict (strɪkt) *adj.* 嚴格的

reliable (rɪˈlaɪəbl̩) *adj.* 可信賴的

solve (sɑlv) *v.* 解決　　kind (kaɪnd) *n.* 種類

hence (hɛns) *adv.* 因此　　sorrow (ˈsɑro) *n.* 悲傷

graduate (ˈgrædʒʊˌet) *v.* 畢業

keep in touch with *sb.* 與某人保持連絡

口説能力測驗詳解

* 請在15秒內完成並唸出下列自我介紹的句子，請開始：

My seat number is ___(複試座位號碼後5碼)___ , and my
registration number is ___(初試准考證號碼後5碼)___ .

一、朗讀短文

請先利用1分鐘的時間閱讀下面的短文，然後在2分鐘內以正常的速度，
清楚正確的朗讀下面的短文。

　　Bats perform an important ecological function throughout
the world. They eat millions of harmful insects yearly. In
fact, the food a bat eats every night amounts to one quarter
of its own body weight. Scientists have observed a single
colony of Arizona bats eat up to 35,000 pounds of insects
every night. That's the equivalent weight of 34 elephants.

　　在全世界，蝙蝠有一項重要的生態功能。牠們每年吃掉數百萬
隻害蟲。事實上，一隻蝙蝠每晚所吃的食物，重達其體重的四分之
一。科學家觀察到，一個亞歷桑那州的蝙蝠群，每晚吃掉重達三萬
五千磅的昆蟲。那相當於三十四隻大象的重量。

【註】bat (bæt) n. 蝙蝠　　perform (pɚˋfɔrm) v. 執行
ecological (ˏikəˋlɑdʒɪkḷ) adj. 生態的
function (ˋfʌŋkʃən) n. 功能；職責
harmful (ˋhɑrmfəl) adj. 有害的　　insect (ˋɪnsɛkt) n. 昆蟲
yearly (ˋjɪrlɪ) adv. 每年　　*amount to* 總計達
quarter (ˋkwɔrtɚ) n. 四分之一　　weight (wet) n. 重量
observe (əbˋzɝv) v. 觀察　　single (ˋsɪŋgḷ) adj. 單一的
colony (ˋkɑlənɪ) n. 群體　　*up to* 多達
equivalent (ɪˋkwɪvələnt) adj. 相等的

　　We have an adopted daughter whom we love dearly.
We also have a biological child.　To us there is absolutely
no difference between them and of course we wish our
adopted daughter felt that way, too.　We strongly believe
if we can steer her through this emotionally stormy period
of adolescence, she will not give another thought to finding
her own mother.

　　我們有一個養女，我們非常愛她。我們也有一個親生的小孩。
對我們而言，他們兩個並沒有差別，當然，我們希望我們的養女，
也有相同的感受。我們堅信，如果我們能引導她走過這段情緒起伏
很大的青春期，她將不再會有尋找親生母親的念頭。

【註】 adopted (ə'dɑptɪd) *adj.* 領養的
　　　 dearly ('dɪrlɪ) *adv.* 非常地
　　　 biological (ˌbaɪə'lɑdʒɪkḷ) *adj.* 生物的；與生命過程有關的
　　　 biological child 親生的小孩
　　　 absolutely (ˌæbsə'lutlɪ) *adv.* 絕對地
　　　 strongly ('strɔŋlɪ) *adv.* 強烈地
　　　 steer (stɪr) *v.* 引導
　　　 emotionally (ɪ'moʃənḷɪ) *adv.* 在感情方面
　　　 stormy ('stɔrmɪ) *adj.* 激烈的；變動多的
　　　 period ('pɪrɪəd) *n.* 時期
　　　 adolescence (ˌædḷ'ɛsṇs) *n.* 青春期
　　　 give thought to 考慮

The most effective way to help a manufacturer sell more of his products is advertising. Nowadays there are countless advertising agencies, which deal with all the publicity that will promote the sale of goods. Advertisements are found on TV, in newspapers and magazines. In return, the manufacturer has to pay the agency for their services. And it is indeed a large amount of money.

　　幫廠商賣出更多的產品，最有效的方法，就是廣告。現在有無數的廣告公司，專門處理所有產品促銷的宣傳活動。我們在電視、報紙和雜誌上，都可看到廣告。製造商必須付費給廣告公司，以回報他們所提供的服務。而那的確是一筆很龐大的金額。

【註】 effective〔əˋfɛktɪv〕*adj.* 有效的
　　　　manufacturer〔͵mænjəˋfæktʃərə〕*n.* 製造業者；廠商
　　　　advertising〔ˋædvə͵taɪzɪŋ〕*n.* 廣告
　　　　countless〔ˋkauntlɪs〕*adj.* 無數的
　　　　agency〔ˋedʒənsɪ〕*n.* 代理商
　　　　deal with 處理　　publicity〔pʌbˋlɪsətɪ〕*n.* 宣傳
　　　　promote〔prəˋmot〕*v.* 促進　　goods〔gudz〕*n. pl.* 商品
　　　　advertisement〔͵ædvəˋtaɪzmənt〕*n.* 廣告
　　　　in return 作為交換　　indeed〔ɪnˋdid〕*adv.* 的確
　　　　a large amount of 大量的

二、回答問題

這個部分共有 10 題。題目已事先錄音，每題經由耳機播出二次，不印在試題冊上。第 1 至 5 題，每題回答時間 15 秒；第 6 至 10 題，每題回答時間 30 秒。每題播出後，請立即回答。回答時，不一定要用完整的句子，但請在作答時間內儘量的表達。

※ 第 1 至第 5 題，每題回答時間 15 秒。

1. Q : What did you see on your way here?

你在來這裡的路上看見了什麼？

A1 : Since I took the MRT, the only thing I saw was people rushing to go places and bumping into each other.

因為我搭捷運，所以我只看到人群在來往穿梭中，相互碰撞。

A2 : The traffic outside is just terrible. I saw nothing but cars. There were also several accidents. I hope nobody got hurt.

外面的交通實在是太糟糕了。除了車子以外，什麼都看不到。還有幾起車禍。我希望沒有人受傷。

A3 : I saw a funeral procession on the way here. I felt sad for the family of the deceased.

我來這裡的路上看到有人出殯。我替往生者的家屬感到難過。

【註】 1. **MRT** 捷運 (= *Mass Rapid Transit*)
rush (rʌʃ) v. 匆忙　　**bump into** 碰撞
nothing but 只是 (= *only*)
funeral ('fjunərəl) n. 葬禮
procession (prə'sɛʃən) n. 行列
deceased (dɪ'sist) adj. 死的　　**the deceased** 死者

2. Q : Do you have any tips for making friends?

　　　你對於交朋友有任何建議嗎？

A1 : The best way to make friends is to be an outgoing, friendly person yourself.

　　　交朋友最好的方法，就是自己要是個活潑外向而且友善的人。

A2 : In order to make friends with others, you must show interest in what is important to others.

　　　要和別人交朋友，你必須對別人所重視的事物感興趣。

A3 : By finding people with the same hobbies as yourself, you can make a lot of friends.

　　　找到和你有相同嗜好的人，就能交到許多朋友。

3. Q : What is your favorite TV program?　Why?

　　　你最喜歡的電視節目是什麼？為什麼？

A1 : My favorite TV show is "The X-Files." This show is about two FBI agents going around investigating unexplainable occurrences.　Besides dealing with aliens, they also have to expose the government's conspiracy.　I always find conspiracy theories fascinating.

【註】 2. tip (tɪp) *n.* 勸告；秘訣
　　　　outgoing ('aʊt,goɪŋ) *adj.* 外向的　hobby ('hɑbɪ) *n.* 嗜好
　　　3. file (faɪl) *n.* 檔案　　agent ('edʒənt) *n.* 密探
　　　　investigate (ɪn'vɛstə,get) *v.* 調查
　　　　unexplainable (,ʌnɪk'splenəbl̩) *adj.* 無法解釋的
　　　　occurrence (ə'kɝəns) *n.* 事件
　　　　deal with 來往；打交道　　alien ('elɪən) *n.* 外星人

> 我最喜歡的電視節目是「X 檔案」。這個節目是講兩位聯邦調查局探員，到處去調查無法解釋的事件。除了處理外星人事件之外，他們還要揭發政府的陰謀。我一向都對陰謀論很感興趣。

A2：I like to watch "Super Sunday." The host and hostess of the show are among my favorite TV personalities. They also make the show funny and entertaining.

> 我喜歡看「超級星期天」。這個節目的男女主持人，是我最喜歡的電視人物中的兩個。他們也讓這個節目旣好玩又有趣。

A3：Since I don't watch TV, I don't have a favorite TV program.

> 因爲我不看電視，所以我沒有最喜歡的電視節目。

---

4. Q : Here is a situation: You are taking a bath, and suddenly you hear someone shout, "Fire!" What would you do?

> 現在這裡有一個狀況：你正在洗澡，突然聽見有人大喊：「失火了！」你會怎麼做？

A1：I would wrap a towel around myself and run out of the house as quickly as I could.

> 我會用毛巾把自己包住，然後儘快跑離房子。

【註】 3. expose (ɪkˈspoz) v. 揭穿（秘密）
conspiracy (kənˈspɪrəsɪ) n. 陰謀
theory (ˈθiərɪ) n. 理論
fascinating (ˈfæsn̩ˌetɪŋ) adj. 吸引人的
host (host) n. 節目主持人
hostess (ˈhostɪs) n. 女主持人
personality (ˌpɝsn̩ˈælətɪ) n. 人物
entertaining (ˌɛntɚˈtenɪŋ) adj. 有趣的

A2 : I would first put on some clothes, make sure everyone is safely evacuated and escape as quickly as possible.

我會先穿上衣服，確定每個人都安全撤離後，再趕緊逃離。

A3 : I would try to find the fire and put it out.

我會試著找到火源，把它撲滅。

5. Q : Describe your childhood. 描述一下你的童年。

A1 : I had an extremely happy childhood. My parents nurtured and loved me very much.

我有個非常快樂的童年。我的父母養育我，也很愛我。

A2 : I was the center of my parents' attention. Then, when I was 7 years old, my baby sister replaced me as the favorite child.

我曾是父母注意力的焦點。然後，七歲時，我的小妹妹取代了我，成了最受寵的小孩。

A3 : My childhood was not special at all. I don't really remember anything spectacular about it.

我的童年一點也不特別。我不太記得有過什麼特別的事。

【註】 4. ***take a bath*** 洗澡　　wrap〔ræp〕v. 包；裹
towel〔taʊl〕n. 毛巾　　evacuate〔ɪ'vækjʊˌet〕v. 撤離
escape〔ə'skep〕v. 逃走　　***put out*** 撲滅

5. replace〔rɪ'ples〕v. 取代
extremely〔ɪk'strimlɪ〕adv. 非常
nurture〔'nɝtʃɚ〕v. 養育
spectacular〔spɛk'tækjələ〕adj. 引人注目的；驚人的

※ 第 6 至第 10 題，每題回答時間 30 秒。

6. Q ： Some people say it is difficult to gain happiness. What do you think?

　　有人說，得到快樂很困難。你有什麼看法？

　 A1 ： I don't think it's very difficult to gain happiness. Just follow your heart and do what you want to do; this way, you will naturally be happy.

　　我不認為要得到快樂很困難。只要順著自己的心意，去做自己想要的事；這樣你自然就會快樂。

　 A2 ： It is absolutely right. We see depressed people every day. Everybody is killing each other and fighting each other. If it were easy to be happy, then we would all live in a better world.

　　完全正確。我們每天都看到沮喪的人。大家都互相殘殺或打鬥。如果很容易就能快樂的話，那麼我們就能活在一個更美好的世界了。

---

7. Q ： If you were an English teacher, how would you teach your students?

　　如果你是英文老師，你會如何教導學生？

【註】 6. gain〔gen〕v. 獲得
　　　 follow〔'falo〕v. 遵照；聽從
　　　 depressed〔dɪ'prɛst〕adj. 沮喪的

A1 : First, I would promote free thinking. The students need to have their own thoughts, instead of letting the teacher tell them how to think. Then, I would promote free talking. Every student can voice his or her opinion, but it has to be done in English.

> 首先,我會提倡自由思考。學生必須要有自己的想法,而不是讓老師告訴他們如何去思考。然後,我會提倡自由發言。每個學生都可以發表自己的意見,但是必須用英文。

A2 : I would encourage my students to keep a diary in English. That way, they can practice their writing skills. I would also have them do impromptu speeches once a month to practice their speaking skills.

> 我會鼓勵學生用英文寫日記。那樣一來,他們可以練習寫作技巧。同時,我會要他們每個月做一次即席演講,來練習他們的口說技巧。

A3 : I would start and give my full support to an English club and ask my foreign friends to come and speak with my students regularly. I would also encourage them to speak English as much as possible.

> 我會成立並全力支持英文社團,而且我會請我的外國朋友們,定期來和我的學生交談。我也會鼓勵他們儘量說英文。

【註】 7. promote (prə'mot) v. 提倡
diary ('daɪərɪ) n. 日記
impromptu (ɪm'prɑmptu) adj. 即席的
give support to 支持~ club (klʌb) n. 社團

8. Q : Talk about the benefits of exercise.

請談一下運動的益處。

A1 : Exercising helps you maintain a healthy life. So you can live a longer, happier life.

運動能幫助你維持健康。這樣你能活得更久，更快樂。

A2 : Being overweight is a common problem in modern society. The reason is that people eat too well and do not exercise. If a person does not exercise, then his weight will increase; thus making him fat and ugly. That would be bad.

體重過重是現代社會常見的問題。原因是人們吃得太好，卻不運動。如果一個人不運動，體重就會增加；因而變得又胖又醜。這樣就不好了。

9. Q : Describe your family. 描述一下你的家庭。

A1 : My family consists of my parents, my two younger sisters, and myself. My father is a lawyer and my mother is a high school teacher. My little sister is a kindergarten teacher in America. And my baby sister is currently in college studying to be a lawyer.

我的家庭成員有父母，兩個妹妹和我。我的父親是個律師，而母親是個高中老師。大妹妹在美國當幼稚園老師。小妹現在讀大學，準備當律師。

【註】　8. overweight (ˈovɚˌwet) *n.* 體重過重
ugly (ˈʌglɪ) *adj.* 醜的
9. ***consist of*** 由～組成
kindergarten (ˈkɪndɚˌgɑrtn̩) *n.* 幼稚園
currently (ˈkɝəntlɪ) *adv.* 目前；現在

A2：I am the only child in my family. I always wanted to have an older brother or sister whom I can look up to. Instead, my parents provided me with their love and guidance.

我是家中的獨子。我總是想要有哥哥或姊姊能做榜樣。不過，我的父母很愛我並指引我。

A3：There is really nothing to say about my family. My parents are divorced and my mother raised me single-handedly. I never really got to know my father, so I can't really say anything about him.

我的家庭實在是沒什麼好說的。我的父母離婚，母親獨立扶養我。我其實沒什麼機會了解我的父親，所以我實在講不出什麼有關於他的事。

---

10. Q ：Most people think Taipei's traffic is terrible. Can you suggest a way to improve it?

大部分的人認為台北的交通很糟糕。你能建議一個方法來改善這種情況嗎？

A1：Too many cars and too many motor scooters is the cause of the traffic problem. We should encourage people to utilize the public transit system.

太多的汽車和機車是造成交通問題的原因。我們應該鼓勵大家使用大眾運輸系統。

【註】　9. *look up to* 尊敬　　guidance ('gaɪdn̩s) *n.* 指導
　　　　divorce (də'vɔrs) *v.* 離婚　　raise (rez) *v.* 養育
　　　　single-handedly ('sɪŋgl̩'hændɪdlɪ) *adv.* 獨立地

　　　10. scooter ('skutɚ) *n.* 速克達機車
　　　　utilize ('jutl̩,aɪz) *v.* 利用　　transit ('trænsɪt) *n.* 運輸

A2：We should increase the tax on cars and motor scooters. This will make people think twice about buying cars. Therefore, we can reduce the number of cars out on the streets.

我們應該加重汽機車的稅。這樣大家在買車之前，就會三思而後行。而街上汽車的數量也就可以減少了。

A3：People in Taiwan do not really obey traffic laws. The fine for traffic violation should be increased. When everybody becomes a law-abiding citizen, the traffic situation will improve.

台灣人不太遵守交通規則。違反交通規則的罰款應該提高。當每個人都變成守法的市民時，交通狀況就會改善了。

【註】　10. tax〔tæks〕*n.* 稅　　reduce〔rɪ'djus〕*v.* 減少
　　　　fine〔faɪn〕*n.* 罰款　　violation〔͵vaɪə'leʃən〕*n.* 違反
　　　　law-abiding〔'lɔə͵baɪdɪŋ〕*adj.* 守法的
　　　　citizen〔'sɪtəzn̩〕*n.* 市民

三、看圖敘述

下面有一張圖片及五個相關的問題，請在 1 分半鐘內完成作答。作答時，請直接回答，不需將題號及題目唸出。首先請利用 30 秒的時間看圖及問題。

1. 這是什麼地方？

This place looks like a beach with lots of people.

這裡看起來像是個有很多人的海灘。

2. 圖片中的人在做什麼？

Some people are swimming and others are sunbathing.

有些人在游泳，有些在做日光浴。

3. 你喜歡去海灘嗎？

I don't like to go to the beach. 我不喜歡去海灘。

4. 為什麼？

Every time I go to the beach, I get sand all over me. The sea water also leaves me with a sticky feeling.

我每次去海灘，身上都沾滿了砂子。海水也會讓我覺得身上黏黏的。

5. 請詳細敘述圖片中的人、事、物。

This is a beach. There are lots of people swimming and sunbathing. There is a wooded area surrounding the beach. Partly covered by the trees is the changing room. In the front of the picture is a family of four. The mother is walking away from the water and her son is following her carrying a float. The father is walking towards the little boy and the elder son is wanting to go back into the water.

這裡是個海灘。有很多人在游泳，以及做日光浴。海灘周圍有一片樹林。更衣室有一部分被樹掩蓋了。在相片前面是一家四口人。媽媽正在走離水邊，而她的兒子拎著一個游泳圈跟在後面。爸爸正走向小男孩，而大兒子想要回到水裡。

【註】 4. sunbathe (ˈsʌnˌbeð) v. 做日光浴　sticky (ˈstɪkɪ) adj. 黏的
　　　 5. wooded (ˈwʊdɪd) adj. 有森林的
　　　　 surround (səˈraʊnd) v. 環繞　 *changing room* 更衣室
　　　　 float (flot) n. 游泳圈

*請將下列自我介紹的句子再唸一遍，請開始：

My seat number is ___(複試座位號碼後5碼)___ , and my registration number is ___(初試准考證號碼後5碼)___ .

⊕EPT® 全民英語能力分級檢定測驗
中級寫作能力測驗答案紙

座位號碼：＿＿＿＿＿＿＿＿＿＿＿＿＿　　　試卷別：＿＿＿＿＿＿＿

第一部分請由第1行開始作答，請勿隔行書寫。

25

30

35

40

中級英語檢定測驗第二階段

寫作口說能力測驗④

寫作能力測驗

一、中譯英（40 分）

說明：請將下列的一段中文翻譯成通順、達意且前後連貫的英文。

　　有句有名的中國諺語說：「讀萬卷書，行萬里路」。它告訴我們讀書愈多，就知道愈多世界上所發生的事。無疑地，書籍是知識的基本來源，但是，若我們只讀書，而忘了要體驗外在的世界，我們將會錯過生命所要提供及教導我們的樂趣及教訓。

二、英文作文（60 分）

說明：請依下面所提供的文字提示寫一篇英文作文，長度約一百二十字（8 至 12 個句子）。作文可以是一個完整的段落，也可以分段。（評分重點包括內容、組織、文法、用字遣詞、標點符號、大小寫）

提示：網路的使用率越來越普遍。請寫一篇文章說明網路帶來的影響及好處。

口說能力測驗

＊請在15秒內完成並唸出下列自我介紹的句子，請開始：

My seat number is ___(複試座位號碼後5碼)___ , and my
registration number is ___(初試准考證號碼後5碼)___ .

一、朗讀短文

請先利用1分鐘的時間閱讀下面的短文，然後在2分鐘內以正常的
速度，清楚正確的朗讀下面的短文。

Want to know if you are really nervous? Clasp
the palms of your hands together. How do they feel?
If your skin feels chilly, you are really nervous. Get
your body moving, trot around the block, or do some
sit-ups. You will feel the warmth coming back and
you will feel much better. And before you face the
challenge that frightens you, remember to take a
deep breath.

＊　　　　　＊　　　　　＊

A chance Internet encounter between a man and
a woman hundreds of miles apart in America ended
with the police rushing to the woman's apartment
after she declared in cyberspace that she was trying
to kill herself. The woman was chatting with a man

over the Internet when she stated that she wanted to end her life. The only information the man had was that she lived in Boston. With that information, the police were able to find and save the woman.

*　　　　*　　　　*

The fax machine is one of the most useful modern telecommunications inventions. By using it, people can send text or even illustrations instantly to anyone within reach of another fax machine anywhere. However, a fax is no substitute for a letter when it comes to making a formal approach to a potential customer, replying to an inquiry, or the like.

二、回答問題

這個部分共有 10 題。題目已事先錄音，每題經由耳機播出二次，不印在試題冊上。第 1 至 5 題，每題回答時間 15 秒；第 6 至 10 題，每題回答時間 30 秒。每題播出後，請立即回答。回答時，不一定要用完整的句子，但請在作答時間內儘量的表達。

三、看圖敘述

下面有一張圖片及一個相關的問題,請在 1 分半鐘內完成作答。
作答時,請直接回答,不需將題號及題目唸出。首先請利用 30 秒
的時間看圖及問題。

1. 請詳細地敘述圖中的人、事、物,並運用自己的想像力,對
   其背後的故事加以補充。

*請將下列自我介紹的句子再唸一遍,請開始:

My seat number is ___(複試座位號碼後 5 碼)___, and my
registration number is ___(初試准考證號碼後 5 碼)___.

寫作口説能力測驗 ④ 詳解

寫作能力測驗詳解

一、中譯英（40分）

　　有句有名的中國諺語說：「讀萬卷書，行萬里路」。它告訴我們讀書愈多，就知道愈多世界上所發生的事。無疑地，書籍是知識的基本來源，但是，若我們只讀書，而忘了要體驗外在的世界，我們將會錯過生命所要提供及教導我們的樂趣及教訓。

　　A famous Chinese proverb goes, "Reading a thousand books is like traveling a thousand miles." It tells us that the more we read, the more we will learn about what is going on in the world. Without doubt, the basic source of our knowledge comes from books; however, if we only read and fail to experience the world outside, we will miss the fun and lessons provided and taught to us by life.

【註】 proverb〔'prɑvɝb〕*n.* 諺語
go on 發生　　*without doubt* 無疑地
source〔sors〕*n.* 來源
fail to 未能；沒有　　lesson〔'lɛsn̩〕*n.* 教訓；課程
provide〔prə'vaɪd〕*v.* 提供

二、**英文作文**（60分）

【作文範例】

    Today, with the easy access to the Internet, searching for information has never been easier. It doesn't matter if you are looking for information for a school paper, or simply looking for someone's phone number. People all over the world can use the Internet to find information.

    The Internet has also changed the way we communicate forever. Most notably, and the most widely used, is email. Email allows us to write to our friends and receive letters from anyone in the world who has access to a computer and telephone line. Plus, we can send and receive our mail instantly across the globe rather than sometimes waiting weeks for a letter to arrive. And now, with heated competition among computer manufacturers, buying and using a computer is easy and cheap. In fact, some companies even give you free access to the Internet and make their money from advertisers instead of you.

    Even though we communicate differently from our parents, you can be sure that it will be much different for our children, too.

【註】access ('æksɛs) n. 使用
internet ('ɪntə,nɛt) n. 網際網路
search (sɜtʃ) v. 搜尋
information (,ɪnfə'meʃən) n. 資訊
look for 尋找　　simply ('sɪmplɪ) adv. 只；單單地
phone number 電話號碼
change (tʃendʒ) v. 改變　　way (we) n. 方式
paper ('pepə) n. 報告
communicate (kə'mjunə,ket) v. 溝通
forever (fə'ɛvə) adv. 永遠
notably ('notəblɪ) adv. 值得注意地
wildly ('waɪdlɪ) adv. 廣大地
email ('i,mel) n. 電子郵件 (= *e-mail*)
allow (ə'laʊ) v. 允許　　receive (rɪ'siv) v. 接收
plus (plʌs) adv. 此外 (= *besides*)
instantly ('ɪnstəntlɪ) adv. 立即地
globe (glob) n. 地球　　*rather than* 而不是
heated ('hitɪd) adj. 激烈的
competition (,kɑmpə'tɪʃən) n. 競爭
manufacturer (,mænjə'fæktʃərə) n. 製造業者；廠商
in fact 事實上　　free (fri) adj. 免費的
advertiser (,ædvə'taɪzə) n. 刊登廣告者
instead of 而不是　　*even though* 雖然
sure (ʃʊr) adj. 確定的

口説能力測驗詳解

* 請在 15 秒內完成並唸出下列自我介紹的句子，請開始：

My seat number is ___(複試座位號碼後 5 碼)___, and my
registration number is ___(初試准考證號碼後 5 碼)___.

一、朗讀短文

請先利用 1 分鐘的時間閱讀下面的短文，然後在 2 分鐘內以正常的速度，
清楚正確的朗讀下面的短文。

Want to know if you are really nervous? Clasp the palms
of your hands together. How do they feel? If your skin feels
chilly, you are really nervous. Get your body moving, trot
around the block, or do some sit-ups. You will feel the
warmth coming back and you will feel much better. And
before you face the challenge that frightens you, remember
to take a deep breath.

想知道你是否真的緊張嗎？把手掌緊握在一起。有什麼感覺？如
果你的皮膚感覺冷冷的，你的確很緊張。動一動身體，到街上去走
走，或做些仰臥起坐。你將會再度覺得溫暖，而且感覺好多了。在你
面對令你恐懼的挑戰之前，記得要深呼吸。

【註】 nervous ('nɜvəs) adj. 緊張的　　clasp (klæsp) v. 緊握
palm (pɑm) n. 手掌　　chilly ('tʃɪlɪ) adj. 冷的
trot (trɑt) v. 快走　　sit-up ('sɪtʌp) n. 仰臥起坐
warmth (wɔrmθ) n. 溫暖　　face (fes) v. 面對
challenge ('tʃælɪndʒ) n. 挑戰
frighten ('fraɪtn) v. 使害怕
take a deep breath 做深呼吸

　　A chance Internet encounter between a man and a woman hundreds of miles apart in America ended with the police rushing to the woman's apartment after she declared in cyberspace that she was trying to kill herself. The woman was chatting with a man over the Internet when she stated that she wanted to end her life. The only information the man had was that she lived in Boston. With that information, the police were able to find and save the woman.

　　有一男一女相隔好幾百英哩，在美國的網路上邂逅，由於女方在網上透露自殺的意圖，最後以警方衝進那女子的公寓作爲收場。當那名女子正在網上與這名男子聊天，她表示她想結束自己的生命。他所知道的唯一訊息就是，她住在波士頓。得知這個消息，警方才能找到那名女子，救了她一命。

【註】　chance〔tʃæns〕adj. 偶然的
　　　　Internet〔'ɪntɚ͵nɛt〕n. 網際網路
　　　　encounter〔ɪn'kaʊntɚ〕n. 相遇
　　　　apart〔ə'pɑrt〕adv. 遠離地
　　　　end with 以～作爲結束　　rush〔rʌʃ〕v. 衝進
　　　　declare〔dɪ'klɛr〕v. 表示
　　　　cyberspace〔͵saɪbɚ'spes〕n. 電腦網路組成的空間
　　　　chat〔tʃæt〕v. 聊天　　state〔stet〕v. 說

The fax machine is one of the most useful modern telecommunications inventions. By using it, people can send text or even illustrations instantly to anyone within reach of another fax machine anywhere. However, a fax is no substitute for a letter when it comes to making a formal approach to a potential customer, replying to an inquiry, or the like.

　　傳眞機是現代通訊設備中，最有用的發明之一。藉由傳眞機，人們可以立即把文字資料，甚至挿圖，傳送給在任何地點，在傳眞機附近的人。然而，傳眞無法取代一般信件，例如，在與可能成爲公司顧客的人做正式接洽時，回覆詢問時，或類似的狀況等。

【註】 telecommunications (ˌtɛləkəˌmjunəˈkeʃənz) *n.* 電信
　　　 invention (ɪnˈvɛnʃən) *n.* 發明
　　　 text (tɛkst) *n.* 正文；原文
　　　 illustration (ɪˌlʌsˈtreʃən) *n.* 挿圖
　　　 instantly (ˈɪnstəntlɪ) *adv.* 立刻地
　　　 within reach of 在～附近
　　　 substitute (ˈsʌbstəˌtjut) *n.* 代替物
　　　 when it comes to 一提到
　　　 formal (ˈfɔrml̩) *adj.* 正式的
　　　 approach (əˈprotʃ) *n.* 接洽；交涉
　　　 potential (pəˈtɛnʃəl) *adj.* 潛在的；有可能的
　　　 reply (rɪˈplaɪ) *v.* 回覆　　　 inquiry (ɪnˈkwaɪrɪ) *n.* 詢問
　　　 or the like 或其他同類者

二、回答問題

這個部分共有 10 題。題目已事先錄音，每題經由耳機播出二次，不印在試題冊上。第 1 至 5 題，每題回答時間 15 秒；第 6 至 10 題，每題回答時間 30 秒。每題播出後，請立即回答。回答時，不一定要用完整的句子，但請在作答時間內儘量的表達。

※ 第 1 至第 5 題，每題回答時間 15 秒。

1. Q ： Could you briefly introduce yourself?

　　　你能不能簡單地介紹你自己？

A1 ： My name is Leo. I am currently working as an English teacher. I wasn't always an English teacher, though. I was a police officer for a few years. I enjoy reading a lot. And my favorite hobbies are fishing and scuba diving.

　　　我的名字是 Leo。我現在的工作是英文老師。但我以前並不是英文老師。我曾經當過幾年警察。我很喜歡看書。而且我最喜歡的嗜好是釣魚和潛水。

A2 ： My name is Wang Shu-ping. I am a freshman at National Taiwan Normal University. I am majoring in English and I hope that I can be an English teacher.

　　　我叫王書平。我是國立師範大學一年級的學生。我主修英文，而且希望能成爲英文老師。

【註】　1. briefly (ˈbriflɪ) *adv.* 簡單地；簡短地
　　　　introduce (ˌɪntrəˈdjus) *v.* 介紹
　　　　currently (ˈkɝəntlɪ) *adv.* 目前；現在
　　　　scuba (ˈskubə) *n.* 水肺　　diving (ˈdaɪvɪŋ) *n.* 潛水
　　　　freshman (ˈfrɛʃmən) *n.* 高一新生；大一新生
　　　　major (ˈmedʒɚ) *v.* 主修

A3 : My name is Wu Pei-wen, but my friends call me Kevin. I am a freshman at Yen-Ping High School. I was born in Tainan.

> 我叫吳沛文，但我朋友都叫我 Kevin。目前就讀延平中學一年級。我出生於台南。

---

2. Q : Where do you think is the best place to prepare for a test? 你認為在哪裡準備考試最好？

A1 : I think that home is the best place for me to prepare for a test. I feel most comfortable in my own room and my family knows not to disturb me.

> 我認為家裡是準備考試最好的地方。在我自己的房間裡，我覺得最舒服，而且家人也不會打擾我。

A2 : I can never stay at home to study. There are just too many distractions for me. I like to study for a test in the quietness of a library.

> 我無法待在家裡念書，因為有太多讓我分心的事物。我喜歡在安靜的圖書館裡準備考試。

A3 : I think studying at McDonald's is best for me. I can have a discussion with my classmates and I can also eat and drink there.

> 我認為在麥當勞念書最好。我可以和同學一起討論，也可以吃東西、喝飲料。

【註】 2. prepare (prɪˋpɛr) v. 準備
　　　disturb (dɪˋstɝb) v. 打擾；擾亂
　　　distraction (dɪˋstrækʃən) n. 令人分心的事
　　　quietness (ˋkwaɪətnɪs) n. 安靜
　　　discussion (dɪˋskʌʃən) n. 討論

3. Q ： Describe today's weather.　描述一下今天的天氣。

　　A₁ ： The weather today is just wonderful.　It is sunny and warm with an occasional breeze.　It's not too hot. It's not too cold.　It's just right.

　　　　今天的天氣很棒。天氣晴朗，很溫暖，偶爾會吹來一陣微風。天氣不太熱，不太冷，剛剛好。

　　A₂ ： It is raining outside.　It has been raining for one month straight now and it doesn't look like it is going to let up any time soon.

　　　　外面正在下雨。已經連續下了一個月了，而且看起來，雨不會很快就停。

　　A₃ ： It is really hard to believe that we are living in Taiwan with weather like today's.　It is so cold, I thought I was in Alaska or something.　It is even snowing on Yang-min Mountain.

　　　　住在台灣會遇到像今天這樣的天氣，真的很難令人相信。天氣好冷，我覺得好像在阿拉斯加那樣的地方。甚至連陽明山都下雪了。

---

4. Q ： What kind of fruit do you like best?　Why?

　　　　你最喜歡什麼水果？為什麼？

【註】 3. describe〔dɪˋskraɪb〕*v.* 敘述
　　　 weather〔ˋwɛðə〕*n.* 天氣
　　　 wonderful〔ˋwʌndəfəl〕*adj.* 很棒的
　　　 sunny〔ˋsʌnɪ〕*adj.* 晴朗的
　　　 occasional〔əˋkeʒənḷ〕*adj.* 偶爾的
　　　 breeze〔briz〕*n.* 微風
　　　 straight〔stret〕*adv.* 連續不斷地　　*let up* 停止
　　　 or something 諸如此類的

A1 : I love to eat watermelons, especially during summer time. They are sweet and refreshing. And most importantly, they are a great source of fluids.

我愛吃西瓜，特別是在夏天的時候。西瓜又甜，又讓人感到清爽。而且最重要的是，西瓜是很棒的補充水份的來源。

A2 : I love apples. People always say, "An apple a day keeps the doctor away." I am a firm believer of that saying. I think that eating apples every day is very good for your health.

我喜歡蘋果。大家都說：「一天一顆蘋果，可以遠離醫生。」我非常相信這個諺語。我認為每天吃蘋果有益健康。

---

5. Q : What do you think is the most important thing in your life? 你認為什麼是你生命中最重要的？

A1 : The most important thing in my life would be my family. In times of need, my family is there to support me 100% and they never let me down.

我生命中最重要的是我的家人。在我有需要時，家人總會百分之百地支持我，而且從不讓我失望。

【註】 4. watermelon ('wɔtə,mɛlən) *n.* 西瓜
refreshing (rɪ'frɛʃɪŋ) *adj.* 使人身心爽快的
most importantly 最重要的是
source (sors) *n.* 來源　　fluid ('fluɪd) *n.* 液體
firm (fɜm) *adj.* 堅定的　　saying ('seɪŋ) *n.* 諺語
health (hɛlθ) *n.* 健康
5. support (sə'port) *v.* 支持　　***let sb. down*** 令某人失望

A2 : My car is very important to me. It is so important to me that I will not let anybody touch it. Without it, I am nothing. So I will take care of it like it is my own child.

> 對我而言，我的車子很重要。重要到我不會讓任何人碰它。沒有車子，我就什麼也不是。所以我會好好照顧它，待它如同自己的小孩。

A3 : Right now, the most important thing for me is to pass the Intermediate English Proficiency Test. I will not be able to rest well until I pass the test.

> 現在對我來說，最重要的，就是要通過中級英語檢定測驗。要直到通過測驗，我才能好好地休息。

※ 第 6 至第 10 題，每題回答時間 30 秒。

6. Q : Please describe an embarrassing experience you have had.

> 請描述你曾經有過的尷尬經驗。

A1 : One time I saw a very beautiful girl. I was so busy looking at her that I ran into a light pole. The impact was so great, it knocked me out cold for a couple of minutes. The beautiful girl I was watching ended up calling an ambulance for me.

【註】 5. *take care of* 照顧　　pass (pæs) v. 通過
6. embarrassing (ɪmˈbærəsɪŋ) adj. 尷尬的
run into 撞上　　pole (pol) n. 桿
impact (ˈɪmpækt) n. 撞擊力
great (grɛt) adj. 巨大的　　*knock out* 撞昏
cold (kold) adv. 完全地　　*end up* 結果~
ambulance (ˈæmbjələns) n. 救護車

有一次，我看到一個非常漂亮的女孩。我忙著看她，所以撞上路燈。因爲撞擊力太大，我昏倒了好幾分鐘。那位漂亮的女孩，最後幫我叫了救護車。

A2 : I finally got a date with my dream girl. We went to an expensive restaurant and had a great evening. When the bill came, I realized that I had left my wallet at home. The girl paid for our meal. That was the first and the last time we went out.

我終於能和我的夢中情人約會。我們去一間昂貴的餐廳，而且一起渡過愉快的夜晚。當帳單來時，我發現我竟然把皮夾忘在家裡。結果那頓飯由那女孩付帳。那次是我們第一次，也是最後一次的約會。

7. Q : Who is the person that influences you most in your life? Why?

在你的一生中，誰影響你最深？爲什麼？

A1 : My father influenced me the most in my life. He is a kind and generous person who works very hard, so my family and I can have whatever we want. He taught me the values of good work ethics as well as honesty and loyalty.

【註】 6. date〔det〕n. 約會的對象
　　　dream〔drim〕adj. 夢一般完美的；理想的
　　　bill〔bɪl〕n. 帳單　　realize〔'rɪə,laɪz〕v. 發現
　　　wallet〔'wɑlɪt〕n. 皮夾　　meal〔mil〕n. 一餐
　　7. values〔'veljʊz〕n. pl. 價值觀
　　　ethics〔'ɛθɪks〕n. 道德準則
　　　loyalty〔'lɔɪəltɪ〕n. 忠誠

在我的一生中，父親影響我最深。他是個仁慈又慷慨的人，他很認真地工作，所以我們一家人生活不虞匱乏。他教導我正確的工作道德、誠實和忠誠的價值觀。

A2: My mother influenced me greatly. She is the backbone of our family and she is always there to help me when I have a problem.

我母親對我的影響很深。她是我們全家的支柱，而且當我有任何問題時，她總會幫助我。

---

8. Q : Some people say watching too much TV is not good. What do you think?

有人說電視看太多不好。你認為呢？

A1: Of course, watching too much TV is bad for you. It makes people lazy and turns them into couch potatoes. People should spend more time reading instead of watching TV.

電視看太多當然不好。那會使人懶散，而且會使人成為整天躺在沙發上看電視的懶人。人們應該多花一點時間閱讀，而不是看電視。

【註】 7. influence ('ɪnfluəns) v. 影響
greatly ('gretlɪ) adv. 極；非常地
backbone ('bæk'bon) n. 支柱

8. lazy ('lezɪ) adj. 懶散的　　***turn into*** 變成
couch potato 整天躺在沙發上看電視的懶人
instead of 而不是

A2：Watching TV is both entertaining and educational. Also, it is a great source of news around the world. You can watch the news on TV as it happens. So I think it is good to watch TV.

看電視既有娛樂性，也有教育性。而且也是得知世界新聞很好的來源。你能從電視上看到正在發生的新聞。所以我認爲看電視很好。

9. **Q**：It is very hot outside. Which would you rather do, go swimming or stay indoors?

外面天氣很熱。你寧願去游泳，還是待在室內？

A1：I'd love to go swimming, and I would swim to cool myself down when it is very hot outside. It is also a very good exercise. On top of that, I can get a beautiful tan.

我會想去游泳，而且當外面很熱的時候，我會去游泳，讓自己涼快涼快。游泳也是很好的運動。除此之外，我能把皮膚曬成美麗的古銅色。

【註】 8. entertaining (ˌɛntɚˈtenɪŋ) adj. 有娛樂效果的
　　　　educational (ˌɛdʒəˈkeʃənḷ) adj. 有教育性的
　　　　great (gret) adj. 很好的
　　　　happen ('hæpən) v. 發生
　　　9. indoors ('ɪnˈdorz) adv. 在室內
　　　　exercise ('ɛksɚˌsaɪz) n. 運動
　　　　on top of 除了～之外（還有）
　　　　tan (tæn) n. (膚色) 古銅色

A2 : I think I would rather stay indoors. I can not stand heat. I would turn on the air-conditioner to full blast and stay inside to read or watch TV.

我認爲我會寧願待在室內。我無法忍受熱。我會把冷氣開到最強，待在室內看書或看電視。

10.Q : What is your expectation of college life?

你對大學生涯有什麼期待？

A1 : I am really looking forward to entering college, because I can study my favorite subject. Besides, I can meet a lot of girls and make them all my girlfriends, but only the pretty ones.

我很期待上大學，因爲我可以研讀我最喜歡的科目。此外，我可以認識很多女生，讓她們全部都變成我的女朋友，可是要漂亮的才可以。

【註】 9. stand〔stænd〕*v.* 忍受　　　heat〔hit〕*n.* 熱
　　　　air-conditioner 冷氣機
　　　　blast〔blæst〕*n.*（一陣）強風　　*full blast* 猛吹
　　　10. college〔'kɑlɪdʒ〕*n.* 大學　　*look forward to* 期待
　　　　enter〔'ɛntɚ〕*v.* 進入　　subject〔'sʌbdʒɪkt〕*n.* 科目

三、看圖敘述

下面有一張圖片及一個相關的問題，請在 1 分半鐘內完成作答。作答時，請直接回答，不需將題號及題目唸出。首先請利用 30 秒的時間看圖及問題。

1. 請詳細地敘述圖中的人、事、物，並運用自己的想像力，對其背後的故事加以補充。

It was a cold Sunday morning in December. A little girl went to the park by her house to play. The park is inside the city near some very tall buildings. The little girl got there and met up with some of her friends. They decided to go to the playground to play on the slide. Two boys are on the platform getting ready to ride the slide, while the girl is sliding down the slide happily. The grandmother of the boys decided to walk off of the platform because she could not fit into the opening of the slide. Overall, the children had a wonderful day playing in the park.

　　這是十二月一個寒冷的星期天早上。有個小女孩到她家附近的公園去玩。公園位於城市中，附近有一些很高的建築物。小女孩到那裏，遇見了幾個朋友。他們決定到公園內的遊樂場，去玩溜滑梯。有兩個男孩在平台上準備溜滑梯，而女孩正快樂地溜下滑梯。男孩們的祖母決定走下平台，因爲滑梯太小了，她坐不下。大體而言，孩子們在公園裏玩耍，渡過美好的一天。

【註】　1. *meet up with*　偶然碰見
　　　　　playground ('ple,graʊnd) *n.* 遊樂場
　　　　　slide (slaɪd) *n.* 滑梯
　　　　　platform ('plæt,fɔrm) *n.* 平台
　　　　　fit into 容得下　　opening ('opənɪŋ) *n.* 洞；口
　　　　　overall ('ovɚ,ɔl) *adv.* 大體而言

＊請將下列自我介紹的句子再唸一遍，請開始：

My seat number is ＿＿(複試座位號碼後 5 碼)＿＿, and my registration number is ＿＿(初試准考證號碼後 5 碼)＿＿.

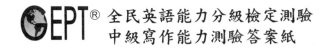
座位號碼：＿＿＿＿＿＿＿＿＿＿　　　試卷別：＿＿＿＿＿＿

第一部分請由第1行開始作答，請勿隔行書寫。

_____

_____

_____

_____

_____

_____

_____

_____

_____

_____

_____

_____

_____

_____

_____

_____

_____

_____

_____

_____

_____

_____

第二部分請翻至第2頁作答

25

30

35

40

中級英語檢定測驗第二階段

寫作口說能力測驗⑤

寫作能力測驗

一、中譯英（40分）

說明：請將下列的一段中文翻譯成通順、達意且前後連貫的英文。

　　網際網路在現在的社會中非常地流行。我們能上網購物，甚至能交女朋友。我的好朋友就是在網路上交了一個女朋友。他們現在已經結婚了。

二、英文作文（60分）

說明：請依下面所提供的文字提示寫一篇英文作文，長度約一百二十字（8至12個句子）。作文可以是一個完整的段落，也可以分段。（評分重點包括內容、組織、文法、用字遣詞、標點符號、大小寫）

提示：每個人都有他們所喜歡做的運動。請寫一篇文章說明

　　（1）你喜歡的運動；

　　（2）為什麼。

口說能力測驗

* 請在15秒內完成並唸出下列自我介紹的句子，請開始：

My seat number is ___(複試座位號碼後5碼)___ , and my registration number is ___(初試准考證號碼後5碼)___ .

一、朗讀短文

請先利用1分鐘的時間閱讀下面的短文，然後在2分鐘內以正常的速度，清楚正確的朗讀下面的短文。

　　Acid rain is not merely an irritation to human beings; it has become a global ecological crisis. The more the scientists investigate acid rain, the more damaging they find it to be to our precious lakes, rivers, forests and wildlife. Some species, both on land and in water, are wiped off the face of the earth by acid rain.

*　　　　　*　　　　　*

　　Have you ever heard of an oxygen bar where you can breathe in oxygen? Owing to the polluted air in the city, people don't get as much oxygen as they used to. Now you can just walk into a bar and put a tube in your nose. The oxygen enters the bloodstream and saturates the air sacs around the heart. Then the heart doesn't have to work as hard to get oxygen.

*　　　　　*　　　　　*

There were no speed limits when the first roads were built in the U.S. Then the number of cars grew. It was safer to have all the cars riding at about the same speed. Before 1973, the speed limit on most roads was 65 miles an hour. Suddenly, the gas supply began to drop. Saving gas became important. One answer was to make a new speed limit of 55 miles an hour.

二、回答問題

這個部分共有 10 題。題目已事先錄音,每題經由耳機播出二次,不印在試題冊上。第 1 至 5 題,每題回答時間 15 秒;第 6 至 10 題,每題回答時間 30 秒。每題播出後,請立即回答。回答時,不一定要用完整的句子,但請在作答時間內儘量的表達。

三、看圖敘述

下面有一張圖片及一個相關的問題，請在 1 分半鐘內完成作答。作答時，請直接回答，不需將題號及題目唸出。首先請利用 30 秒的時間看圖及問題。

1. 請詳細地敘述圖中的人、事、物，並運用自己的想像力，對其背後的故事加以補充。

＊請將下列自我介紹的句子再唸一遍，請開始：

My seat number is ＿＿（複試座位號碼後 5 碼）＿＿, and my
registration number is ＿＿（初試准考證號碼後 5 碼）＿＿.

寫作口說能力測驗 ⑤ 詳解

寫作能力測驗詳解

寫作能力測驗詳解

一、中譯英（40分）

　　網際網路在現在的社會中非常的流行。我們能上網購物，甚至能交女朋友。我的好朋友就是在網路上交了一個女朋友。他們現在已經結婚了。

　　The Internet is very fashionable in modern society. We can go online to do some shopping, and even find a girlfriend online.　A good friend of mine met his girlfriend on the Internet.　They are now married.

【註】 Internet〔'ɪntɚ,nɛt〕*n.* 網際網路
　　　fashionable〔'fæʃənəbl〕*adj.* 流行的
　　　modern〔'mɑdɚn〕*adj.* 現代的
　　　society〔sə'saɪətɪ〕*n.* 社會
　　　do some shopping 購物
　　　online〔'ɑn,laɪn〕*adv.* 連線地；在網上
　　　married〔'mærɪd〕*adj.* 結婚的

二、英文作文（60分）

【作文範例】

  Every person has his or her favorite sport. The reasons differ from person to person. Some people like exciting and competitive sports, and some like recreational sports. Out of all those different kinds of sports, my favorite is skiing.

  I became interested in skiing when I was 12 years old. My parents and I were visiting my aunt in America. She took us on a ski trip. It was the first time I had ever seen and felt snow. My mother enrolled me into a four-hour skiing lesson. After the lesson, I was able to roam around the slopes like a miniature professional skier. The experience was new and wonderful. Ever since then, I have never missed any opportunity to go skiing. The sensation of skiing down the slopes is indescribable. I always imagine myself to be James Bond getting out of harm's way. The adrenaline rush only enhances the sensation, which makes me want to do it over and over again.

　　Due to its sub-tropical weather, it is almost impossible for us to go skiing in Taiwan. However, both Japan and Korea offer excellent snow and slopes for skiing. I am really anticipating my next ski trip.

【註】 competitive (kəm'pɛtətɪv) *adj.* 競爭的
　　　recreational (ˌrɛkrɪ'eʃənl̩) *adj.* 娛樂的
　　　ski (ski) *v. n.* 滑雪
　　　visit ('vɪzɪt) *v.* 拜訪　　aunt (ænt) *n.* 阿姨
　　　trip (trɪp) *n.* 旅行　　lesson ('lɛsn̩) *n.* 課程
　　　enroll (ɪn'rol) *v.* 登記；使入學
　　　roam (rom) *v.* 漫遊　　slope (slop) *n.* 斜坡
　　　miniature ('mɪnɪətʃə) *adj.* 小型的
　　　professional (prə'fɛʃənl̩) *adj.* 專門的
　　　wonderful ('wʌndəfəl) *adj.* 令人驚奇的
　　　ever since then 從那時起
　　　opportunity (ˌɑpə'tunətɪ) *n.* 機會
　　　sensation (sɛn'seʃən) *n.* 感覺；感受
　　　sensation (sɛn'seʃən) *n.* 感覺
　　　indescribable (ˌɪndɪ'skraɪbəbl̩) *adj.* 難以形容的
　　　imagine (ɪ'mædʒɪn) *v.* 想像
　　　out of harm's way 安全地
　　　adrenaline (æd'rɛnl̩ɪn) *n.* 腎上腺素
　　　enhance (ɪn'hæns) *v.* 加強
　　　over and over again 一次又一次
　　　sub-tropical (sʌb'trɑpɪkl̩) *adj.* 亞熱帶的
　　　impossible (ɪm'pɑsəbl̩) *adj.* 不可能的
　　　excellent ('ɛksl̩ənt) *adj.* 極棒的
　　　anticipate (æn'tɪsəˌpet) *v.* 期待

口說能力測驗詳解

* 請在 15 秒內完成並唸出下列自我介紹的句子，請開始：

My seat number is ___(複試座位號碼後 5 碼)___ , and my
registration number is ___(初試准考證號碼後 5 碼)___ .

一、朗讀短文

請先利用 1 分鐘的時間閱讀下面的短文，然後在 2 分鐘內以正常的速度，
清楚正確的朗讀下面的短文。

  Acid rain is not merely an irritation to human beings;
it has become a global ecological crisis. The more the
scientists investigate acid rain, the more damaging they
find it to be to our precious lakes, rivers, forests and
wildlife. Some species, both on land and in water, are
wiped off the face of the earth by acid rain.

  酸雨不僅是使人類感到厭煩的問題，也已成為全球的生態危
機。科學家對酸雨的研究愈深入，就會發現，酸雨對我們珍貴的
湖泊、河川、森林和野生動植物，所造成的傷害愈來愈嚴重。有
些種類的生物，不論是陸地上或水中的生物，都因酸雨而絕種。

【註】 ***acid rain*** 酸雨 merely ('mɪrlɪ) adv. 僅僅
  irritation (ˌɪrə'teʃən) n. 令人煩躁的事物
  human beings 人類 global ('globl̩) adj. 全球的
  ecological (ˌɛkə'lɑdʒɪkl̩) adj. 生態的
  crisis ('kraɪsɪs) n. 危機 investigate (ɪn'vɛstəˌget) v. 研究
  damaging ('dæmɪdʒɪŋ) adj. 具破壞力的
  precious ('prɛʃəs) adj. 珍貴的 forest ('fɔrɪst) n. 森林
  wildlife ('waɪldˌlaɪf) n. 野生動植物
  species ('spiʃɪz) n. 種（生物） ***wipe off*** 完全毀掉

Have you ever heard of an oxygen bar where you can breathe in oxygen? Owing to the polluted air in the city, people don't get as much oxygen as they used to. Now you can just walk into a bar and put a tube in your nose. The oxygen enters the bloodstream and saturates the air sacs around the heart. Then the heart doesn't have to work as hard to get oxygen.

你曾經聽說過可以去那裡吸氧氣的氧氣吧台嗎？由於都市中的空氣污染，人們所呼吸到的氧氣，已不如過去那麼多。現在你只要走進氧氣吧台，把管子接到鼻子上，氧氣就能進入血液中，充滿心臟周圍的氣囊。那樣心臟就不用那麼費力地去獲得氧氣了。

【註】 oxygen (ˈɑksədʒən) n. 氧　　breathe (brið) v. 呼吸
owing to 由於　　polluted (pəˈlutɪd) adj. 受污染的
tube (tjub) n. 管子
bloodstream (ˈblʌd͵strim) n. 血液
saturate (ˈsætʃə͵ret) v. 使充滿　　*air sac* 氣囊

There were no speed limits when the first roads were built in the U.S. Then the number of cars grew. It was safer to have all the cars riding at about the same speed. Before 1973, the speed limit on most roads was 65 miles an hour. Suddenly, the gas supply began to drop. Saving gas became important. One answer was to make a new speed limit of 55 miles an hour.

美國最早期的道路在建造時，並沒有速度限制。然後車子的數量愈來愈多。要所有的車子以相同的速度行駛，是比較安全的。在一九七三年以前，大部份道路的速限是六十五英哩。突然間，汽油的供給量突然開始減少。節省汽油就變得非常重要。其中的一個解決方法，就是規定新的速限，改為時速五十五英哩。

【註】 *speed limit* 速限　　ride〔raɪd〕v. 行駛（車輛）
gas〔gæs〕n. 汽油　　supply〔sə'plaɪ〕n. 供給
drop〔drɑp〕v. 下降；減少　　save〔sev〕v. 節省

二、回答問題

這個部分共有 10 題。題目已事先錄音，每題經由耳機播出二次，不印在試題冊上。第 1 至 5 題，每題回答時間 15 秒；第 6 至 10 題，每題回答時間 30 秒。每題播出後，請立即回答。回答時，不一定要用完整的句子，但請在作答時間內儘量的表達。

※ 第 1 至第 5 題，每題回答時間 15 秒。

1. Q : How did you get here?

你是怎麼來的？

A1 : I rode my bicycle to the MRT station by my house. Then, I rode the MRT to NTU Station. From there on, I walked.

我騎腳踏車到我家附近的捷運站。然後我坐捷運到台大站。從那裡走過來。

A2 : I took the bus here.

我搭公車來的。

【註】 1. *NTU* 台灣大學（= *National Taiwan University*）

2. Q : What is the first thing you do when you wake up in
　　　the morning?

　　　你早上起來所做的第一件事是什麼？

A1 : The first thing I do when I wake up is take a long,
　　　hot shower. Showering in the morning wakes me up.

　　　我起床後所做的第一件事，就是洗個很久的熱水澡。早上
　　　洗澡會讓我清醒過來。

A2 : I usually go running for at least 5 kilometers when I
　　　wake up. Exercising in the morning really clears my
　　　head and gives me energy for the rest of the day.

　　　我起床後通常會去跑步，至少五公里。早上運動會使我的
　　　頭腦清醒，而且讓我一整天都充滿活力。

3. Q : What do you do?

　　　你是做什麼的？

A1 : I am a high school student.

　　　我是個高中生。

junior high school student 國中生	banker 銀行家
elementary school student 小學生	lawyer 律師
college student 大專生	engineer 工程師
teacher 教師	housewife 家庭主婦

【註】 2. shower (ˈʃaʊɚ) *n.* 淋浴
　　　　clear one's head 使某人清醒

　　　3. banker (ˈbæŋkɚ) *n.* 銀行家　　lawyer (ˈlɔjɚ) *n.* 律師
　　　　engineer (ˌɛndʒəˈnɪr) *n.* 工程師
　　　　housewife (ˈhaʊsˌwaɪf) *n.* 家庭主婦

4. Q : Where would you rather be right now? Why?

你現在寧願在什麼地方？為什麼？

A1 : I'd rather be at home sleeping. Taking this test is really exhausting for me. I need to get my beauty sleep.

我寧願待在家裡睡覺。考這個試使我筋疲力盡。我需要睡個美容覺。

A2 : I have not eaten lunch yet and I am very hungry. I'd rather be sitting in a restaurant eating a big bowl of beef noodles.

我很餓，還沒有吃午餐。我寧願坐在餐廳裡，吃一大碗牛肉麵。

5. Q : What kind of food do you like to eat? Why?

你喜歡吃哪種食物？為什麼？

A1 : I like to eat Chinese food and my mother is the best cook. I can not stand any other kinds of food. I guess I'll be out of luck when I travel abroad.

我喜歡吃中國菜，而且我媽媽是最好的廚師。我無法忍受其它種類的食物。我想我如果出國的話，就倒大霉了。

Italian food 義大利菜	fast food 速食
Japanese food 日本料理	Mexican food 墨西哥菜

【註】 4. exhausting (ɪgˋzɔstɪŋ) *adj.* 令人筋疲力盡的
bowl (bol) *n.* 碗　beef (bif) *n.* 牛肉
noodle (ˋnudḷ) *n.* 麵

5. *out of luck* 倒霉　abroad (əˋbrɔd) *adv.* 到國外

※ 第 6 至第 10 題，每題回答時間 30 秒。

6. Q ： What is your educational background?

你的教育背景是什麼？

A1 ： I graduated with a bachelor degree in English from National Taiwan University.

我畢業於台灣大學，並得到英文學士學位。

A2 ： I am currently a freshman at Yen-Ping High School.

我現在是延平中學的高一學生。

A3 ： I am a senior at Ching-Hua University, majoring in math.

我是清華大學數學系的四年級學生。

7. Q ： Have you ever traveled abroad?　Where?　Why?

你有沒有出過國？去哪裏？為什麼會出國？

A1 ： I have been to America several times.　I went there to visit with friends.

我去過美國幾次。我去那裡是為了拜訪朋友。

A2 ： I have never been out of the country before.　That's because I have this incredible fear of flying.

我從來沒有出過國。那是因為我很怕搭飛機。

【註】　6. background ('bæk,graund) n. 背景
　　　　 bachelor ('bætʃələ) n. 學士　　degree (dɪ'gri) n. 學位
　　　　 currently ('kɜəntlɪ) adv. 目前
　　　　 senior ('sinjə) n. 大四學生
　　　 7. incredible (ɪn'krɛdəbḷ) adj. 令人難以相信的
　　　　 fly (flaɪ) v. 搭飛機

8. Q : Are you annoyed when you hear a cellular phone in a movie theater? Why?

你在電影院裡聽見手機響，會不會覺得生氣？爲什麼？

A1 : I will be very annoyed if I hear a cellular phone in a theater. I went to the theater to see a movie, not to hear a cellular phone; also it may distract me.

在電影院裡聽到手機響，會令我非常生氣。我去電影院是爲了看電影，而不是聽手機，還有聽到手機響，可能會使我分心。

9. Q : Do you keep up with current events? How?

你有沒有注意時事的發展？怎麼注意？

A1 : I have been keeping up with current events by reading the newspaper and watching CNN every day.

我每天都會看報紙，以及看 CNN 來注意時事的動向。

10. Q : Do you think you can pass this test? Why?

你覺得你會通過這個測驗嗎？爲什麼？

A1 : I think I can pass this test with flying colors, because I am very confident of my English abilities.

我認爲我會成功地通過考試，因爲我對我的英文能力非常有自信。

【註】　8. annoyed (ə'nɔɪd) adj. 生氣的　*cellular phone* 手機
distract (dɪ'stræk) v. 使分心

9. *keep up with* 跟上　*current events* 時事
keep up with current events 對時事消息靈通

10. *with flying colors* 成功地

三、看圖敘述

下面有一張圖片及一個相關的問題，請在 1 分半鐘內完成作答。作答時，請直接回答，不需將題號及題目唸出。首先請利用 30 秒的時間看圖及問題。

1. 請詳細地敘述圖中的人、事、物，並運用自己的想像力，對其背後的故事加以補充。

　　This is a picture of a battle.　Four soldiers went on a patrol in the jungle.　They made contact with some enemy soldiers and a fierce battle began.　The four soldiers found a trench and used it for cover.　A soldier wearing a helmet sat down in the trench with his back against the wall.　He looked like he was badly wounded. Two soldiers were hit and killed.　One is lying on the ground in the trench and the other is slumped over. The only soldier remaining tried to repel the enemy by shooting high and staying low inside the trench.

　　　這是一張戰場上的照片。有四名軍人在叢林裡巡邏。他們遇到了一些敵軍，於是展開一場激烈的戰鬥。那四名軍人找到了一個壕溝，而且用它來做掩護。一個頭戴鋼盔的士兵坐在壕溝裡，背緊靠著溝壁。他看起來好像身受重傷。兩個士兵已經陣亡了。一個倒在壕溝裡，而另一個則臥倒在壕溝邊。唯一存活的士兵試著要擊退敵人，用壕溝來做掩護，高舉著槍射擊。

【註】1. battle (ˈbætl̩) n. 戰爭　　soldier (ˈsoldʒɚ) n. 軍人
　　　　patrol (pəˈtrol) n. 巡邏　　jungle (ˈdʒʌŋgl̩) n. 叢林
　　　　fierce (fɪrs) adj. 激烈的　　trench (trɛntʃ) n. 壕溝
　　　　cover (ˈkʌvɚ) v. 掩護　　helmet (ˈhɛlmɪt) n. 頭盔
　　　　against (əˈgɛnst) prep. 靠著
　　　　badly (ˈbædlɪ) adv. 嚴重地
　　　　wounded (ˈwundɪd) adj. 受傷的
　　　　slump (slʌmp) v. 倒下
　　　　remain (rɪˈmen) v. 持續；依然
　　　　repel (rɪˈpɛl) v. 擊退　　enemy (ˈɛnəmɪ) n. 敵人
　　　　shoot (ʃut) v. 射擊

*請將下列自我介紹的句子再唸一遍，請開始：

My seat number is ＿＿(複試座位號碼後5碼)＿＿, and my
registration number is ＿＿(初試准考證號碼後5碼)＿＿.

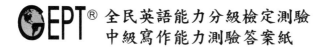

全民英語能力分級檢定測驗
中級寫作能力測驗答案紙

單位號碼：_____　　試卷別：_____

第一部分請由第1行開始作答，請勿隔行書寫。

_____
_____
_____
_____
_____
_____
_____
_____
_____
_____
_____
_____
_____
_____
_____
_____
_____
_____
_____
_____
_____
_____

第二部分請翻至第2頁作答

25

30

35

40

中級英語檢定測驗第二階段

寫作口說能力測驗⑥

寫作能力測驗

一、中譯英（40 分）

說明：請將下列的一段中文翻譯成通順、達意且前後連貫的英文。

　　　我們與別人溝通有幾種方法，如手勢、臉部表情和語言。然而，無疑地，語言是最重要的一種方法。世界上約有三千種語言，其中很多種只有少數人在使用。假使沒有語言，你認為今天的世界會像什麼呢？

二、英文作文（60 分）

說明：請依下面所提供的文字提示寫一篇英文作文，長度約一百二十字（8 至 12 個句子）。作文可以是一個完整的段落，也可以分段。（評分重點包括內容、組織、文法、用字遣詞、標點符號、大小寫）

提示：電話幾乎是每個家庭裡都有的一項科技產品。請寫一篇文章說明電話的重要性。

口說能力測驗

*請在 15 秒內完成並唸出下列自我介紹的句子，請開始：

My seat number is ___(複試座位號碼後 5 碼)___, and my

registration number is ___(初試准考證號碼後 5 碼)___.

一、朗讀短文

請先利用 1 分鐘的時間閱讀下面的短文，然後在 2 分鐘內以正常的
速度，清楚正確的朗讀下面的短文。

The Central Weather Bureau announced a likely dip in temperatures for Valentine's Day. The temperatures will stay warm today, hovering around 22 degrees Celsius in the north and 27 degrees Celsius in central and southern Taiwan. However, temperatures will drop two or three degrees island wide tomorrow. Residents are advised to bring along their jackets on their Valentine's Day outings.

*　　　　　*　　　　　*

"The Art of Chinese Flower Arranging in the New Millennium" will open today at the National Museum of History in Taipei. Participants in the project being organized by the Chinese Floral Foundation will show

how tradition can be reinterpreted with creativity in the floral arts.　The floral art show will run until Feb. 27. The arrangement will be changed twice.

*　　　　*　　　　*

German researchers have made a breakthrough in the fight against cancer.　According to their report, the new technique will help prevent the radiation overdoses common to cancer treatments and the extra strain they put on the patient.　The technique involves the chemical alteration of small sections of DNA.　Experiments on a variety of tumor tissues have shown that within a short period, 80 percent of cells had accepted the new molecules, which were then able to prevent the further spread of cancerous cells.

二、回答問題

這個部分共有 10 題。題目已事先錄音，每題經由耳機播出二次，不印在試題冊上。第 1 至 5 題，每題回答時間 15 秒；第 6 至 10 題，每題回答時間 30 秒。每題播出後，請立即回答。回答時，不一定要用完整的句子，但請在作答時間內儘量的表達。

三、看圖敘述

下面有一張圖片及四個相關的問題，請在 1 分半鐘內完成作答。
作答時，請直接回答，不需將題號及題目唸出。首先請利用 30 秒
的時間看圖及問題。

1. 這是什麼地方的圖片？
2. 你認為這個地方寬敞嗎？
3. 牆上掛著什麼東西？
4. 如果還有時間，請詳細敘述圖片中的陳列。

*請將下列自我介紹的句子再唸一遍，請開始：

My seat number is ＿＿(複試座位號碼後 5 碼)＿＿, and my
registration number is ＿＿(初試准考證號碼後 5 碼)＿＿.

寫作口說能力測驗 ⑥ 詳解

寫作能力測驗詳解

一、中譯英（40分）

我們與別人溝通有幾種方法，如手勢、臉部表情和語言。然而，無疑地語言是最重要的一種方法。世界上約有三千種語言，其中很多種只有少數人在使用。假使沒有語言，你認為今天的世界會像什麼呢？

　　We have a number of ways to communicate with others, such as gestures, facial expressions and speech. However, there is no doubt that speech is the most important way. There are about three thousand languages in the world, many of which are used only by small groups of people. If there were no languages, what do you think the world would be like?

【註】 gesture (ˈdʒɛstʃɚ) n. 手勢
facial (ˈfeʃəl) adj. 臉部的
expression (ɪkˈsprɛʃən) n. 表情
doubt (daʊt) n. 懷疑　　*no doubt* 無疑地
there is no doubt that + S. + V. ～是無庸置疑的
language (ˈlæŋgwɪdʒ) n. 語言

二、英文作文（60分）

【作文範例】

It would be difficult to imagine modern life without a telephone. It has become an indispensable instrument of communication, saving much time by enabling people to talk to one another over great distances.

The telephone is useful and convenient for many reasons. With the help of the telephone, people can talk to their friends miles away, and business organizations can carry on their activities easily. Furthermore, with modern technology, cellular phones have become an affordable convenience. Today, it is even possible to check your e-mail or the price of a stock through your cell phone.

Most important of all, when there is an emergency, the first thing one thinks of is to get to the phone and ask for help. Therefore, we can say that the telephone was one of the most important and valuable inventions of the 20th century.

【註】imagine〔ɪˋmædʒɪn〕v. 想像

modern〔ˋmɑdɚn〕adj. 現代的

indispensable〔͵ɪndɪsˋpɛnsəbḷ〕adj. 不可或缺的

instrument〔ˋɪnstrəmənt〕n. 工具 (= tool)

communication〔kə͵mjunəˋkeʃən〕n. 聯絡

save〔sev〕v. 節省

distance〔ˋdɪstəns〕n. 距離

useful〔ˋjusfəl〕adj. 有用的

mile〔maɪl〕n. 哩

organization〔͵ɔrgənəˋzeʃən〕n. 組織；機構

carry on 進行　　activity〔ækˋtɪvətɪ〕n. 活動

furthermore〔ˋfɝðɚ͵mor〕adv. 此外

technology〔tɛkˋnɑlədʒɪ〕n. 科技

cellular phone 行動電話 (= *cell phone*)

affordable〔əˋfɔrdəbḷ〕adj. 負擔得起的

possible〔ˋpɑsəbḷ〕adj. 可能的

stock〔stɑk〕n. 股票

emergency〔ɪˋmɝdʒənsɪ〕n. 緊急情況

valuable〔ˋvæljuəbḷ〕adj. 珍貴的

invention〔ɪnˋvɛnʃən〕n. 發明

century〔ˋsɛntʃərɪ〕n. 世紀

口說能力測驗詳解

＊請在 15 秒內完成並唸出下列自我介紹的句子，請開始：

My seat number is ＿＿（複試座位號碼後 5 碼）＿＿, and my
registration number is ＿＿（初試准考證號碼後 5 碼）＿＿.

一、朗讀短文

請先利用 1 分鐘的時間閱讀下面的短文，然後在 2 分鐘內以正常的速度，
清楚正確的朗讀下面的短文。

The Central Weather Bureau announced a likely dip in
temperatures for Valentine's Day. The temperatures will
stay warm today, hovering around 22 degrees Celsius in
the north and 27 degrees Celsius in central and southern
Taiwan. However, temperatures will drop two or three
degrees island wide tomorrow. Residents are advised to
bring along their jackets on their Valentine's Day outings.

中央氣象局宣佈，情人節當天，氣溫有可能會下降。今天氣
溫將會維持溫暖，北部地區約攝氏 22 度左右，台灣中、南部地區
則是攝氏 27 度左右。可是，明天全島氣溫將下降 2 或 3 度。我們
建議民眾，在情人節出遊時，要攜帶夾克。

【註】bureau ('bjuro) n. 局
the Central Weather Bureau 中央氣象局
announce (ə'naʊns) v. 宣佈
dip (dɪp) n. (小幅度的) 下降
Valentine's Day 情人節　　hover ('hʌvɚ) v. 盤旋；上下波動
Celsius ('sɛlsɪəs) n. 攝氏　　resident ('rɛzədənt) n. 居民
advise (əd'vaɪz) v. 勸告　　*bring along* 帶在身邊
outing ('aʊtɪŋ) n. 短途旅遊

　　"The Art of Chinese Flower Arranging in the New Millennium" will open today at the National Museum of History in Taipei. Participants in the project being organized by the Chinese Floral Foundation will show how tradition can be reinterpreted with creativity in the floral arts. The floral art show will run until Feb. 27. The arrangement will be changed twice.

　　「千禧年中國插花藝術展」今天將於國立歷史博物館開幕。此展由中國花藝協會主辦，參展者將展示如何在花卉藝術上運用創造力，來重新詮釋傳統。花藝展將舉行至二月廿七日。展覽花卉將更換二次。

【註】 arrange (ə'rendʒ) v. 佈置；排列
　　　 millennium (mə'lɛnɪəm) n. 千禧年
　　　 The National Museum of History 國立歷史博物館
　　　 museum (mju'zɪəm) n. 博物館
　　　 participant (pɚ'tɪsəpənt) n. 參與者
　　　 project ('prɑdʒɛkt) n. 計劃
　　　 organize ('ɔrgən,aɪz) v. 組織
　　　 floral ('florəl) adj. 花的
　　　 foundation (faʊn'deʃən) n. 基金會
　　　 tradition (trə'dɪʃən) n. 傳統
　　　 reinterpret (,riɪn'tɝprɪt) v. 重新解釋
　　　 creativity (,krie'tɪvətɪ) n. 創造力　　 run (rʌn) v. 進行
　　　 arrangement (ə'rendʒmənt) n. 佈置
　　　 twice (twaɪs) adv. 兩次

German researchers have made a breakthrough in the fight against cancer. According to their report, the new technique will help prevent the radiation overdoses common to cancer treatments and the extra strain they put on the patient. The technique involves the chemical alteration of small sections of DNA. Experiments on a variety of tumor tissues have shown that within a short period, 80 percent of cells had accepted the new molecules, which were then able to prevent the further spread of cancerous cells.

德國研究人員在治療癌症上，已有重大突破。根據他們的報告指出，這項新技術將有助於避免放射線過量，那正是癌症治療中常見的問題，以及避免對病人造成的過度負擔。這項技術包括 DNA 小部份的化學變化。對於多種腫瘤組織所做的實驗顯示，在短期內，百分之八十的細胞，接受了新的分子，這樣就能夠避免癌細胞的進一步擴散。

【註】 researcher〔rɪ'sɝtʃɚ〕*n.* 研究人員
breakthrough〔'brek,θru〕*n.* 突破
cancer〔'kænsɚ〕*n.* 癌症　　technique〔tɛk'nik〕*n.* 技術
prevent〔prɪ'vɛnt〕*v.* 防止　　radiation〔,redɪ'eʃən〕*n.* 放射線
overdose〔'ovɚ,dos〕*n.* 過量　　common〔'kɑmən〕*adj.* 常見的
treatment〔'tritmənt〕*n.* 治療　　strain〔stren〕*n.* 負擔；壓力
involve〔ɪn'vɑlv〕*v.* 包括　　chemical〔'kɛmɪkḷ〕*adj.* 化學的
alteration〔,ɔltə'reʃən〕*n.* 變化　　section〔'sɛkʃən〕*n.* 部分
DNA 去氧核糖核酸　　experiment〔ɪk'spɛrəmənt〕*n.* 實驗
a variety of 各式各樣的　　tumor〔'tjumɚ〕*n.* 腫瘤
tissue〔'tɪʃʊ〕*n.* 組織　　cell〔sɛl〕*n.* 細胞
molecule〔'mɑlə,kjul〕*n.* 分子
further〔'fɝðɚ〕*adj.* 更進一步的　　spread〔sprɛd〕*n.* 擴散
cancerous〔'kænsərəs〕*adj.* 癌症的

二、回答問題

這個部分共有 10 題。題目已事先錄音，每題經由耳機播出二次，不印在試題冊上。第 1 至 5 題，每題回答時間 15 秒；第 6 至 10 題，每題回答時間 30 秒。每題播出後，請立即回答。回答時，不一定要用完整的句子，但請在作答時間內儘量的表達。

※ 第 1 至第 5 題，每題回答時間 15 秒。

1. Q ： What languages do you speak?

你會說哪種語言？

A1 : I speak Mandarin, Taiwanese, and English. Mandarin and Taiwanese are my mother tongues, English is my first foreign language. I can also speak a little French and Japanese, as my second and third foreign languages.

我會說國語、台語和英語。國語和台語是我的母語，英語是我的第一外國語。此外，我還會說一點法語和日語，那是我的第二和第三外國語。

2. Q ： Do you have a pet? What is it and what's its name? If not, what pet would you like to have?

你有養寵物嗎？你養什麼寵物，叫什麼名字呢？如果你沒有寵物，你想養什麼呢？

【註】　1. Mandarin〔ˈmændərɪn〕*n.* 國語
　　　　 mother tongue 母語
　　　　 2. pet〔pɛt〕*n.* 寵物

A1 : Yes, I have a pet. It's a dog and its name is Lucky.
It's a white Maltese and looks most healthy, lively
and cute.

　　有，我養了一隻寵物，是一隻狗，名字叫來福。它是一隻
　　白色的馬爾濟斯，看起來很健康、活潑，而且很可愛。

A2 : No, I don't have a pet. My mother doesn't allow me
to keep a pet. I wish I had a cat, because cats are
low maintenance pets and they are very clean.

　　沒有，我沒有養寵物，我媽媽不准我養。我希望養隻貓，
　　因為貓比較不需照顧，而且很愛乾淨。

---

3. Q : What kind of movies do you like best?
　　你最喜歡哪一種電影？

A1 : I like action movies best, because I love excitement.
　　我最喜歡動作片，因為我喜歡刺激。

A2 : I enjoy romances, especially those with heart-throbs.
I'm a sucker for "and they lived happily ever after."
　　我喜歡文藝片，特別是由俊男美女主演的。我最喜歡看到
　　「他們從此以後過著幸福快樂的日子」。

A3 : Thrillers are my favorite.　驚悚片是我的最愛。

【註】 2. lively ('laɪvlɪ) *adj.* 活潑的
　　　　 Maltses (mɔl'tiz) *n.* 馬爾濟斯
　　　　 maintenance ('mentənəns) *n.* 撫養

　　　 3. heart-throb ('hɑrt,θrɑb) *n.* 偶像；迷戀的對象
　　　　 be a sucker for ~ 對~入迷
　　　　 thriller ('θrɪlɚ) *n.* 驚悚片

A4：I love horror movies. 我喜歡看恐怖片。

A5：I prefer comedies. They always relieve me of my tension and relax me.

　　我比較喜歡喜劇片。喜劇片總是能消除我的緊張，讓我放鬆。

A6：I like watching tragedies. I am easily moved to tears.

　　我喜歡看悲劇。我很容易被感動落淚。

4. Q ：How often do you go to the movies?

　　你多久看一次電影？

A1：I go to the movies nearly every weekend. I love to see the latest films Hollywood has to offer.

　　我幾乎每個週末都去看電影。我喜歡看最新的好萊塢電影。

A2：I go see a movie about once a month.

　　我大約一個月看一次電影。

A3：I seldom go to the movies, because I am very busy. Usually I watch videotapes or the reruns on cable TV.

　　我很少去看電影，因為我很忙。通常我都看錄影帶，或第四台重播的影片。

【註】 3. horror（ˈhɑrɚ）n. 恐怖　　comedy（ˈkɑmədɪ）n. 喜劇
　　　　relieve（rɪˈliv）v. 消除　　tension（ˈtɛnʃən）n. 緊張
　　　　tragedy（ˈtrædʒədɪ）n. 悲劇　　move（muv）v. 感動

　　 4. *go to the movies* 去看電影
　　　　latest（ˈletɪst）*adj.* 最新的
　　　　videotape（ˈvɪdɪoˌtep）n. 錄影帶
　　　　rerun（ˈriˌrʌn）n. 重播的電影
　　　　cable TV 有線電視；第四台

5. Q : How do you usually get to school?

你通常怎麼去上學？

A1 : I usually go to school by bus/by MRT/by train/by bicycle/on foot.

我通常坐公車/捷運/火車/騎腳踏車/走路上學。

A2 : Usually, my father or mother drives me to school. This enables me to leave home half an hour later than if I had to take the bus.

通常，我爸爸或媽媽會開車送我上學。這樣我可以比去坐公車晚半小時出門。

A3 : I live in the school dormitory, so it is very convenient for me to go to class. It's just a five-minute walk.

我住在學校宿舍裏，所以上課非常方便。只要走五分鐘就到了。

※ 第 6 至第 10 題，每題回答時間 30 秒。

6. Q : What type of weather do you prefer? Why?

你比較喜歡哪一種天氣？爲什麼？

A1 : I prefer cloudy weather, because it is not that hot and it makes me feel more comfortable. Furthermore, I don't need to use an umbrella to shield me from sun or rain. I feel light and free.

我比較喜歡多雲的天氣，因爲不會那麼熱，讓我覺得比較舒服。此外，我不用撐傘來遮陽或擋雨。感覺輕鬆又自在。

【註】 5. **MRT** 捷運 (= *Mass Rapid Transit*)
dormitory ('dɔrmə,torɪ) *n.* 宿舍

6. furthermore ('fɝðɚ,mor) *adv.* 此外
shield (ʃild) *v.* 保護　　light (laɪt) *adj.* 輕鬆的

A2： I prefer sunny weather, because it always makes me feel energetic and keeps me in high spirits.

我比較喜歡晴天，因為會讓我覺得充滿活力，使我心情很好。

A3： I like rainy days. Though it is not convenient to go outside, rain does give me a feeling of romance. Besides, it is cooler on rainy days and the air seems to be fresher, too.

我喜歡下雨天。雖然外出不方便，但雨天給我一種浪漫的感覺。此外，下雨天比較涼爽，空氣似乎也比較新鮮。

---

7. Q ： What is your favorite season? Why?

你最喜歡哪一個季節？為什麼？

A1： My favorite season is spring, because the weather is warm and the flowers are in bloom. I like the overall feeling of rebirth that comes with spring, and it seems to put a spring in my step.

我最喜歡的季節是春天，因為天氣溫暖，百花盛開。我喜歡隨著春天而來的那種大地回春的感覺，似乎腳步都輕盈了起來。

【註】　6. energetic〔͵ɛnɚ'dʒɛtɪk〕*adj.* 充滿活力的
　　　　in high spirits 心情好
　　　　romance〔ro'mæns〕*n.* 浪漫的氣氛

　　　7. bloom〔blum〕*n.* 花開的狀態　　***in bloom*** 開花
　　　　overall〔'ovɚ͵ɔl〕*adj.* 全面的
　　　　spring〔sprɪŋ〕*n.* 彈性；活力；春天

A2： I like summer best, because I can go swimming at the beach.　And it won't be necessary to put on heavy clothes, so I always feel light and free.　Also I don't like to be cold, and the winter is always cold and miserable.　On the contrary, the summertime is always sunny and warm, except for the occasional rain, which I don't mind at all.

> 我最喜歡夏天，因為我可以到海邊游泳。而且，不必穿厚重的衣物，所以我總是覺得輕鬆自在。並且，我不喜歡冷，而冬天總是又冷又討厭。相反地，夏天總是溫暖而晴朗，除了偶爾下點雨，不過我一點也不介意。

A3： My favorite season is fall, because it's neither too hot nor too cold.　The weather is perfect and makes me feel comfortable.

> 我最喜歡的季節是秋天，因為不會太熱也不會太冷。天氣剛剛好，讓我覺得很舒服。

A4： My favorite season is winter, because Christmas and Chinese New Year are both in wintertime.　Even though there is no snow in Taiwan, I like the scenery of snow in the mountains.　Also I don't like it when it gets really hot.　In the wintertime, it is always nice and cool, which is just the way I like it.

> 我最喜歡的季節是冬天，因為耶誕節和過年都在冬天。即使台灣不下雪，我還是喜歡山上的雪景。並且，我不喜歡天氣熱。冬天一直都很涼爽舒適，我就是喜歡這樣子。

【註】 7. scenery (ˈsinərɪ) n. 風景
　　　　 miserable (ˈmɪzərəbl̩) adj. 惱人的
　　　　 on the contrary 相反地
　　　　 occasional (əˈkeʒənl̩) adj. 偶然的

8. Q ： What do you usually do on a rainy day?

下雨天你通常都做什麼？

A1 ： I usually stay at home, either watching TV or videotapes, sleeping, or spending time with my family, because I think it's a lot of trouble to go outside carrying an umbrella on a rainy day.

我通常待在家裡，看電視或錄影帶、睡覺，或陪伴家人，因為我覺得下雨天出門還要帶傘，很麻煩。

9. Q ： What will you do if you have an afternoon off?

如果你放一個下午的假，你會做什麼？

A1 ： I will go buy a novel and read it at a coffee shop over a cup of coffee.

我會去買本小說，找家咖啡廳，邊喝咖啡邊看書。

A2 ： I will go window shopping or go to the movies with my classmates. I know I should be devoting all my free time to the upcoming JCEE, but sometimes I need a breather.

我會和同學去逛街或看電影。我知道我應該把所有的空閒時間，都拿來準備即將來臨的聯考，但偶爾我也需要休息一下。

【註】 9. *have ~ off* 休假
over〔'ovɚ〕*prep.* 邊~；在~的時候
go window shopping 瀏覽櫥窗
upcoming〔'ʌpˌkʌmɪŋ〕*adj.* 即將來臨的
breather〔'briðɚ〕*n.* 短暫的休息

A3 : I usually go to the library and do some reading. I like to read current periodicals like Reader's Digest and 19th century novels such as Dickens.

我通常到圖書館看書。我喜歡看最新的雜誌,像讀者文摘, 以及十九世紀的小說,如狄更斯的作品。

---

10. Q : What club do you belong to at school? And what do you do at the club?

你在學校參加什麼社團?你在社團裡都做些什麼?

A1 : I belong to the English Conversation Club. I practice English conversation with other club members. Each week one member must make a five-minute speech and then we have a discussion about it.

我參加英語會話社,和其他社員練習英語會話。每週每個 社員都要做一次五分鐘的演講,然後我們會一起討論。

A2 : I am part of the Guitar Club and I learned how to play the guitar. We will soon have a guitar competition, so I am practicing very hard.

我參加吉他社,學習如何彈吉他。我們即將舉行吉他演奏 比賽,所以我正在加緊練習。

【註】 9. current ('kɝənt) *adj.* 現在的
  periodical (ˌpɪrɪ'ɑdɪkḷ) *n.* 期刊;雜誌
  digest ('daɪdʒɛst) *n.* 摘要
  Dickens ('dɪkɪnz) *n.* 狄更斯 (英國小說家)

  10. ***belong to*** 屬於 club (klʌb) *n.* 社團
  make a speech 演講
  competition (ˌkɑmpə'tɪʃən) *n.* 比賽
  participate (pɑr'tɪsəˌpet) *v.* 參加

A3：I participate in the Folk Dance Club.　I think dancing is both interesting and good for health.

我參加土風舞社。我認爲跳舞旣有趣，又有益健康。

A4：I am a member of the Harmonica Club.　Being able to play songs with a harmonica really makes me proud of myself.

我參加口琴社。能夠用口琴吹奏歌曲，眞是令我感到自豪。

【註】　10. folk〔fok〕*adj.* 民俗的
harmonica〔harˋmɑnɪkə〕*n.* 口琴
be proud of 以～爲榮

三、看圖敘述

下面有一張圖片及四個相關的問題，請在 1 分半鐘内完成作答。作答時，請直接回答，不需將題號及題目唸出。首先請利用 30 秒的時間看圖及問題。

1. 這是什麼地方的圖片？

This is a picture of a person's bedroom.

這是某人臥室的圖片。

2. 你認爲這個地方寬敞嗎？

I don't think it is a roomy place.　It seems to be a small bedroom.

我不認爲這個地方寬敞。這個地方看起來是一間蠻小的臥室。

【註】　2. roomy〔ˋrumɪ〕*adj.* 寬敞的

3. 牆上掛著什麼東西？

There are six pictures on the wall, and one of them is a portrait.

牆上有六幅圖畫，其中一幅是某個人的畫像。

Beside the door on the left, there is a towel hanging on the wall. There is also a rack beside the window and there are some things hanging on it.

在左邊的門旁邊，有一條毛巾掛在牆上。窗戶旁邊還有一個架子，上面也掛了一些東西。

4. 如果還有時間，請詳細敘述圖片中的陳列。

The main thing in the bedroom is the bed on the right. There are two pillows and sheets on the bed. By the bed is a chair, and to the left of the chair is a table. Another chair is in front of the door on the left. There is also another door on the right at the foot of the bed.

這個房間主要的東西，就是右邊那張床。床上有兩個枕頭和床單。床邊有一張椅子，椅子的左邊有張桌子。另一張椅子在左邊門前，還有一扇門在床腳右邊。

【註】 3. rack〔ræk〕n. 架子
　　　 4. pillow〔'pɪlo〕n. 枕頭　　sheets〔ʃits〕n. pl. 床單

* 請將下列自我介紹的句子再唸一遍，請開始：

My seat number is ___(複試座位號碼後5碼)___, and my registration number is ___(初試准考證號碼後5碼)___.

⊙EPT® 全民英語能力分級檢定測驗
中級寫作能力測驗答案紙

座位號碼: _____　　　　試卷別: _____

第一部分請由第1行開始作答,請勿隔行書寫。

_____

_____

_____

_____

_____

_____

_____

_____

_____

_____

_____

_____

_____

_____

_____

_____

_____

_____

_____

_____

_____

_____

25

30

35

40

中級英語檢定測驗第二階段

寫作口說能力測驗 ⑦

寫作能力測驗

一、中譯英（40分）

說明：請將下列的一段中文翻譯成通順、達意且前後連貫的英文。

　　　電視有許多不良的影響。很多學生一回家就看電視，以致於疏忽了他們的家庭作業。許多人戴眼鏡，因為他們看太多電視。因此，我們最好愈少看電視愈好。

二、英文作文（60分）

說明：請依下面所提供的文字提示寫一篇英文作文，長度約一百二十字（8至12個句子）。作文可以是一個完整的段落，也可以分段。（評分重點包括內容、組織、文法、用字遣詞、標點符號、大小寫）

提示：當你生病的時候，你通常都怎麼做？你會去看醫生，或是自己去藥房買藥吃呢？請寫一篇文章說明你的做法及理由。

口說能力測驗

*請在15秒內完成並唸出下列自我介紹的句子，請開始：

My seat number is ___(複試座位號碼後5碼)___ , and my
registration number is ___(初試准考證號碼後5碼)___ .

一、朗讀短文

請先利用1分鐘的時間閱讀下面的短文，然後在2分鐘內以正常的
速度，清楚正確的朗讀下面的短文。

The blue crab is a type of crab found off the East
Coast of the United States. It is covered by an armor-
like shell, which makes it a fierce little fighter. It is
unwise to get too close because the blue crab has
two strong claws.

*　　　　　　*　　　　　　*

Police tracked down and rescued a woman who
called for help on her cellular phone after she was
forced into the trunk of her car by a gunman. The
woman's ordeal ended after the suspect crashed on an
exit ramp during a high-speed chase with the police.
The woman, a 24-year-old medical student, suffered
only a bump on the head.

*　　　　　　*　　　　　　*

Many people believe that by studying a person's hand they can tell much about that person. These people are called palmists. They believe that they can tell what will happen to a person by looking at his hand. Palmists believe that each line and crease has a meaning, although they do not all agree as to those meanings.

二、回答問題

這個部分共有 10 題。題目已事先錄音，每題經由耳機播出二次，不印在試題冊上。第 1 至 5 題，每題回答時間 15 秒；第 6 至 10 題，每題回答時間 30 秒。每題播出後，請立即回答。回答時，不一定要用完整的句子，但請在作答時間內儘量的表達。

三、看圖敘述

下面有一張圖片及四個相關的問題，請在 1 分半鐘內完成作答。作答時，請直接回答，不需將題號及題目唸出。首先請利用 30 秒的時間看圖及問題。

1. 這是什麼地方？
2. 圖片中的人在做什麼？
3. 圖片中的背景為何？
4. 如果還有時間，請詳細敘述圖片中的人、事、物。

＊請將下列自我介紹的句子再唸一遍，請開始：

My seat number is ＿＿＿(複試座位號碼後 5 碼)＿＿＿, and my registration number is ＿＿＿(初試准考證號碼後 5 碼)＿＿＿.

寫作口說能力測驗 ⑦ 詳解

寫作能力測驗詳解

一、中譯英（40分）

電視有許多不良的影響。很多學生一回家就看電視，以致於疏忽了他們的家庭作業。許多人戴眼鏡，因為他們看太多電視。因此，我們最好愈少看電視愈好。

Television has many bad influences. A lot of students turn on the television as soon as they get home; hence, they neglect their homework. Many people have to wear glasses because they watch too much TV. Therefore, it would be better if we watch less television.

【註】 television ('tɛlə,vɪʒən) n. 電視
influence ('ɪnfluəns) n. 影響　　*a lot of* 許多
turn on 打開　　*as soon as* 一…就～
hence (hɛns) adv. 因此
neglect (nɪ'glɛkt) v. 忽略
homework ('hom,wɝk) n. 家庭作業
wear (wɛr) v. 戴
glasses ('glæsɪz) n. pl. 眼鏡

二、英文作文（60分）

【作文範例】

　　When I get sick, I usually go see a doctor right away. The doctor will give a diagnosis of my illness and then he will give me some medicine, or if necessary, a shot. After seeing the doctor, I always follow his advice and take the medication regularly, so I can get well soon.

　　Some people have the habit of buying over the counter medicine for their illness from a drugstore. They think that they will save time and money if they treat their illness that way. But I think it is quite risky. If we take the wrong medicine, our illness will worsen and sometimes it may cost us our lives. Therefore, I would rather go see a doctor just to be on the safe side.

【註】 ***right away*** 立刻　　diagnosis (ˌdaɪəg'nosɪs) *n.* 診斷
illness ('ɪlnɪs) *n.* 病　　shot (ʃɑt) *n.* 注射；打針
medication (ˌmɛdɪ'keʃən) *n.* 藥物
regularly ('rɛgjələlɪ) *adv.* 定期地
over the counter medicine 成藥
drugstore ('drʌgˌstor) *n.* 藥房
risky ('rɪskɪ) *adj.* 危險的　　worsen ('wɜsn̩) *v.* 惡化
cost (kɔst) *v.* 使（某人）失去～
to be on the safe side 為了慎重起見

口說能力測驗詳解

* 請在 15 秒內完成並唸出下列自我介紹的句子，請開始：

My seat number is ＿＿（複試座位號碼後 5 碼）＿＿, and my
registration number is ＿＿＿（初試准考證號碼後 5 碼）＿＿＿.

一、朗讀短文

請先利用 1 分鐘的時間閱讀下面的短文，然後在 2 分鐘內以正常的速度，
清楚正確的朗讀下面的短文。

The blue crab is a type of crab found off the East Coast
of the United States. It is covered by an armor-like shell,
which makes it a fierce little fighter. It is unwise to get too
close because the blue crab has two strong claws.

藍蟹是活動於美國東海岸的一種螃蟹。牠身覆如盔甲般的外
殼，這使牠成爲兇猛的小戰士。太接近牠可是不智之舉，因爲藍
蟹有兩隻強而有利的螯。

【註】 crab (kræb) n. 蟹　　armor ('ɑrmɚ) n. 盔甲
shell (ʃɛl) n. 殼　　fierce (fɪrs) adj. 兇猛的
fighter ('faɪtɚ) n. 戰士　　unwise (ʌn'waɪz) adj. 不智的
claw (klɔ) n. (蟹的) 螯

Police tracked down and rescued a woman who called
for help on her cellular phone after she was forced into the
trunk of her car by a gunman. The woman's ordeal ended
after the suspect crashed on an exit ramp during a high-
speed chase with the police. The woman, a 24-year-old
medical student, suffered only a bump on the head.

警方循線追蹤，並救出一名女子。有名持槍的歹徒強迫她進入她車子的後車廂之後，她就打行動電話求救。在警匪高速的追逐戰中，嫌犯撞上出口彎道之後，這名女子的苦難經歷才結束。這位二十四歲的醫學院女學生所受的傷害，只有頭上被撞一個包。

【註】 track〔træk〕v. 追蹤　　rescue〔'rɛskju〕v. 救出
　　　cellular phone 行動電話　　force〔fɔrs〕v. 強迫
　　　trunk〔trʌŋk〕n. 汽車後車廂
　　　gunman〔'gʌn,mæn〕n. 持槍者
　　　ordeal〔ɔr'dil〕n. 痛苦的經驗
　　　suspect〔'sʌspɛkt〕n. 嫌疑犯
　　　crash〔kræʃ〕v. 相撞　　exit〔'ɛksɪt〕n. 出口
　　　ramp〔ræmp〕n. 彎道；交流道　　chase〔tʃes〕n. 追逐
　　　suffer〔'sʌfɚ〕v. 遭受　　bump〔bʌmp〕n. 腫塊

Many people believe that by studying a person's hand they can tell much about that person. These people are called palmists. They believe that they can tell what will happen to a person by looking at a his hand. Palmists believe that each line and crease has a meaning, although they do not all agree as to those meanings.

許多人相信藉由看手相，可以知道一個人的許多事情。這些人被稱為掌相家。他們認為藉由看一個人的掌相，就可知道他未來會發生什麼事。掌相家認為，手掌的每一條紋路都有其意義，雖然他們對紋路意義的詮釋未必相同。

【註】 palmist〔'pɑmɪst〕n. 掌相家
　　　crease〔kris〕n. 皺摺　　*as to* 關於

二、回答問題

這個部分共有 10 題。題目已事先錄音，每題經由耳機播出二次，不印在試題冊上。第 1 至 5 題，每題回答時間 15 秒；第 6 至 10 題，每題回答時間 30 秒。每題播出後，請立即回答。回答時，不一定要用完整的句子，但請在作答時間內儘量的表達。

※ 第 1 至第 5 題，每題回答時間 15 秒。

1. Q ： Do you like to go swimming?　Why?

你喜歡游泳嗎？爲什麼？

A1 ： I enjoy swimming a lot.　It is my favorite sport. Swimming can thoroughly cool a person down.　That way, I can cool myself off and exercise at the same time, killing two birds with one stone.

我很喜歡游泳。那是我最喜歡的運動。游泳能讓人徹底涼快。那樣子，我能讓自己涼快，同時也做了運動，眞是一舉兩得。

A2 ： I don't like to go swimming because I don't know how to swim.　I guess I just never got around to learning how.

我不喜歡游泳，因爲我不會游。我一直都找不到時間去學。

【註】　1. *get around to* 找到時間做
thoroughly ('θɜolɪ) *adv.* 徹底地；完全地
killing two birds with one stone 一舉兩得

2. Q ： Which do you enjoy more, eating out or eating at home? Why?

你比較喜歡在外面吃飯，還是在家吃飯？爲什麼？

A1 ： I hate eating out. You can never tell what you are really eating when you are eating out. I prefer my mother's home cooking.

我很討厭在外面吃飯。在外面吃飯，你總是無法得知，你到底吃了些什麼。我還是比較喜歡我媽媽煮的菜。

A2 ： I eat out all the time. It is fast and convenient. And the most important of all, I don't have to cook.

我都是在外面吃的。既快又方便。最重要的是，我不必自己煮。

———————————————

3. Q ： Do you think recycling is important?

你覺得資源回收重要嗎？

A1 ： Of course recycling is important. The earth's natural resources are limited. If we don't recycle, then the earth's resources will be gone before we know it.

資源回收當然重要。地球的天然資源是有限的。如果我們不回收的話，那麼地球的資源很快就會沒了。

A2 ： I don't really care about recycling. People around us are not really into recycling so why should I care.

我對資源回收不是很關心。因爲我們周圍的人都對資源回收沒興趣，所以我爲什麼要在乎。

【註】 2. *eat out* 在外面吃飯
　　　 3. recycle (rɪˋsaɪkl̩) v. 回收；再利用
　　　 resources (rɪˋsorsɪs) n. pl. 資源
　　　 be into 對～有興趣

4. Q : How much time do you spend on the telephone every day? 你每天要花多少時間講電話？

A1 : I don't talk on the phone much because I don't have any friends.　When I do make phone calls, I spend no more than three minutes each time.

我不是很常講電話，因為我沒有朋友。但是當我講電話時，我不會講超過三分鐘。

A2 : I love to talk on the phone.　I usually spend at least half an hour talking on the phone each time.　I wouldn't know what to do without the telephone.

我很喜歡講電話。我每次至少要花半個鐘頭講電話。要是沒有電話，我會不知所措。

---

5. Q : What would you do if you were eating dinner at a restaurant and found a half eaten cockroach in your food?

如果你在餐廳吃晚餐的時候，在你的食物裡發現一隻被吃掉一半的蟑螂，你會怎麼做？

A1 : The notion of a cockroach in my food is so repulsive.　I would probably throw up.

想到在我的食物裡有蟑螂，真是令人反胃。我大概會吐出來。

【註】 4. *make phone calls* 打電話
　　　 5. cockroach (ˈkɑkˌrotʃ) *n.* 蟑螂
　　　　 notion (ˈnoʃən) *n.* 想法
　　　　 repulsive (rɪˈpʌlsɪv) *adj.* 令人厭惡的
　　　　 throw up 嘔吐

A2: I would call the waiter over and demand to know why this had happened. Then I would go on the Internet and tell the whole world about it.

> 我會把服務生叫過來，並且要求知道，為什麼會發生這種事。然後我會上網告訴全世界的人。

※ 第 6 至第 10 題，每題回答時間 30 秒。

6. Q : Do you have any hobbies? Why?

> 你有沒有任何嗜好？為什麼？

A1 : I enjoy reading a lot. It is my favorite hobby. By reading different books, I can learn many things. Like the ancient Chinese proverb says, "Reading a thousand books is better than traveling a thousand miles." I do believe that by reading a lot, I can broaden my horizons.

> 我很喜歡閱讀。那是我最喜歡的嗜好。藉著閱讀不同種類的書，我可以學到很多東西。正如中國古老的諺語所說：「讀萬卷書勝過行萬里路。」我相信，書讀多一點，能使我增廣見聞。

A2 : My favorite hobby is fishing. It is a challenging but safe activity. When I catch a fish, the sense of achievement is indescribable. Fishing also puts some extra food on the table.

> 我最喜歡的嗜好是釣魚。那是個既有挑戰性，而且又安全的活動。當我釣到魚的時候，那種成就感真是難以形容。並且，釣到的魚還可以加菜。

【註】 6. broaden ('brɔdn̩) v. 增廣
horizons (hə'raɪzn̩z) n.pl. 眼界；見聞
challenging ('tʃælɪndʒɪŋ) adj. 有挑戰性的
indescribable (,ɪndɪ'skraɪbəbl̩) adj. 難以形容的
extra ('ɛkstrə) adj. 額外的

7. Q ： In your opinion, who is the most important person in the 20th century? Why?

以你的觀點，誰是二十世紀最重要的人？爲什麼？

A1 ： I think the most important person in the 20th century is Mikhail Gorbachev. He pushed for the unification of Germany, which caused the democratization of the Soviet Union as well as the rest of Eastern Europe.

我認爲戈巴契夫是二十世紀最重要的人。他推動了東西德統一，導致了蘇聯和東歐國家的民主化。

A2 ： Harry Truman is perhaps the most important person of the 20th century. He made the decision to drop the atomic bomb, a weapon of mass destruction, on Japan; hence, ending World War II.

杜魯門也許是二十世紀最重要的人。他決定在日本投下兩顆具有高度毀滅性的武器，原子彈。因而結束了第二次世界大戰。

8. Q ： What is the craziest thing you have ever done? Would you do it again?

你做過最瘋狂的事是什麼？你還會不會再做一次？

【註】　7. *push for* 強逼　　unification〔͵junəfə'keʃən〕*n.* 統一
democratization〔də͵mɑkrətaɪ'zeʃən〕*n.* 民主化
Soviet Union〔'sovɪɛt'junjən〕*n.* 蘇聯
drop〔drɑp〕*v.* 投下　　atomic〔ə'tɑmɪk〕*adj.* 原子的
bomb〔bɑm〕*n.* 炸彈　　weapon〔'wɛpən〕*n.* 武器
mass〔mæs〕*adj.* 大量的
destruction〔dɪ'strʌkʃən〕*n.* 毀滅

A1 : I went bungee jumping once. It was probably the craziest thing I have ever done. It was so exciting and I would definitely do it again.

　　我有一次去高空彈跳。那大概是我所做過最瘋狂的事。我絕對還會再做一次，因為那實在是太刺激了。

A2 : I am never really into any crazy stunts. But the craziest thing I have ever done would be spending $30,000NT on buying a bicycle. I would never do that again because it almost bankrupted me.

　　我不喜歡做瘋狂的事。但是我所做過最瘋狂的事，是我花了台幣三萬元去買一台腳踏車。我再也不會做那樣的事了，因為我差點因此而破產。

---

9. Q : Have you ever chatted with people on the Internet? Why or why not?

　　你有沒有上網與人聊過天？為什麼有或為什麼沒有？

A1 : I always go on to the Internet to chat with people. It is a way of meeting with people from all over the world. I can talk to people from England and America all at the same time.

　　我經常上網和人聊天。那是一種認識世界各地的人的好方法。我能在同時和在英國的人，以及在美國的人聊天。

【註】　8. *bungee jumping* 高空彈跳　　*be into* 喜歡
　　　　　stunt (stʌnt) *n.* 特技；驚險動作
　　　　　bankrupt ('bæŋkrʌpt) *v.* 使破產
　　　　9. Internet ('ɪntɚˏnɛt) *n.* 網際網路
　　　　　chat (tʃæt) *v.* 聊天

A2： I would like to go on to the Internet, but I can't do that yet. I don't have a computer and I have yet to learn to use a computer. Until then, I'll just have to listen to people talk about Internet chatting.

我會想要上網，但是我現在還不能這麼做。我沒有電腦，而且我也還沒有學會如何使用電腦。在那以前，我只好聽人講關於上網聊天的事。

---

10. Q ： If you won a million dollars, what would you do with it?

你如果贏了一百萬元，你會怎麼用這筆錢？

A1： I would invest the money into the stock market and hopefully double my money.

我會把錢投資在股票上，並且希望能把錢變成兩倍。

A2： I would give the money to my mother. I am sure that she could find a good use for the money.

我會把錢給我媽媽。我相信她一定能好好運用這筆錢。

【註】 10. million ('mɪljən) n. 百萬
invest (ɪn'vɛst) v. 投資
stock (stɑk) n. 股票
market ('mɑrkɪt) n. 市場
hopefully ('hopfəlɪ) adv. 但願
double ('dʌbl̩) v. 使加倍
sure (ʃʊr) adj. 確定的

三、看圖敘述

下面有一張圖片及四個相關的問題，請在 1 分半鐘內完成作答。作答時，請直接回答，不需將題號及題目唸出。首先請利用 30 秒的時間看圖及問題。

1. 這是什麼地方？

   This is an airline counter at the airport.

   這是機場內的一家航空公司櫃檯。

2. 圖片中的人在做什麼？

   The man is crouching to find something in his baggage, and the woman is looking at him.

   那男人蹲下來在行李裡找東西，而那女人正在看著他。

3. 圖片中的背景為何？

   Some clerks in uniform are sitting behind the counter, waiting for passengers to check in. Obviously, they are not very busy because there are not many people in line.

   穿制服的服務人員坐在櫃檯後面，等乘客來辦理登機手續。
   顯然他們並不忙，因為沒有很多人在排隊。

【註】 1. airline (ˈɛr,laɪn) *n.* 航空公司
   counter (ˈkaʊntɚ) *n.* 櫃台
   2. crouch (kraʊtʃ) *v.* 蹲伏　　baggage (ˈbægɪdʒ) *n.* 行李
   3. clerk (klɝk) *n.* 職員　　uniform (ˈjunə,fɔrm) *n.* 制服
   in uniform 穿制服的　　passenger (ˈpæsn̩dʒɚ) *n.* 乘客
   check in 辦理登機手續
   obviously (ˈɑbvɪəslɪ) *adv.* 明顯地　　*in line* 排隊

4. 如果還有時間，請詳細敘述圖片中的人、事、物。

　　There are two people waiting at the check-in counter. Both of them wear heavy coats, so the weather must be cold outside.　As they were about to check in, the man couldn't find his passport and flight ticket.　So he is crouching to unpack his baggage to look for them. Instead of nagging at the man, the woman is just looking at him with a smile.

　　　登機櫃檯有兩個人在排隊。他們兩人都穿著厚重的大衣，所以外面的天氣一定很冷。當他們準備要辦理登機手續時，這個男人找不到他的護照和機票。因此他蹲下來，打開他的行李來尋找。這個女人並沒有對這個男人嘮叨，只是微笑地看著他。

　　　【註】　4. heavy〔ˋhɛvɪ〕adj. 厚重的　**be about to** 即將
　　　　　　　passport〔ˋpæs͵port〕n. 護照
　　　　　　　flight ticket 機票（＝*plane ticket*）
　　　　　　　unpack〔ʌnˋpæk〕v. 打開（行李）
　　　　　　　nag〔næg〕v. 嘮叨

＊請將下列自我介紹的句子再唸一遍，請開始：

　　My seat number is ＿＿（複試座位號碼後5碼）＿＿, and my registration number is ＿＿（初試准考證號碼後5碼）＿＿.

◀» 口說測驗得分祕訣

　　朗讀短文的祕訣是，要一個字一個字的唸，在一分鐘閱讀的時候，不要唸出聲音。如果唸出聲音來，會被監考人員制止，這樣會影響你作答的心情。在開始朗讀的時候，不要急著把短文全部唸完。慢慢的來，儘量清楚的把句子唸出來。就算唸錯了，也不要停下來重唸，要繼續把文章唸完。請放心，時間一定夠。

　　看圖敘述的得分祕訣是，要先把圖片的整體看一遍，了解圖片中所描述的是什麼地方，大體的敘述一遍。之後再針對細節，詳細地敘述圖片中的事物。

GEPT® 全民英語能力分級檢定測驗
中級寫作能力測驗答案紙

座位號碼：＿＿＿＿＿＿＿＿＿＿＿＿　　　試卷別：＿＿＿＿＿＿

第一部分請由第1行開始作答，請勿隔行書寫。

25

30

35

40

中級英語檢定測驗第二階段

寫作口說能力測驗⑧

寫作能力測驗

一、中譯英（40分）

說明：請將下列的一段中文翻譯成通順、達意且前後連貫的英文。

　　昨天我在超級市場買東西的時候，遇見了我的國中同學瑪麗（Mary）。我們已經有十年沒見了。她看起來跟以前完全不同。她比以前瘦多了。我們一起去咖啡館坐了一會。畢竟我們很久沒見了。

二、英文作文（60分）

說明：請依下面所提供的文字提示寫一篇英文作文，長度約一百二十字（8至12個句子）。作文可以是一個完整的段落，也可以分段。（評分重點包括內容、組織、文法、用字遣詞、標點符號、大小寫）

提示：作文題目：

你的名字是溫蒂（Wendy）。你在下星期三要去一家公司面試。但是另一家公司，突然也通知你在同日同時去面試。你不想因為去一家公司面試，而錯過另一個機會。現在請利用下面的格式，寫一封信給新公司，向他們請求更改面試的時間。記住，要先很有禮貌地感謝對方給你一個面試的機會，接著向他們解釋你為什麼要改時間，以及你想要改到什麼時候。不要忘了向對方道謝。

today's date

To whom it may concern,

_____

_____

_____

_____

_____

_____

_____

_____

Sincerely yours,
Wendy

口說能力測驗

＊請在 15 秒內完成並唸出下列自我介紹的句子，請開始：

My seat number is ＿＿（複試座位號碼後 5 碼）＿＿, and my
registration number is ＿＿（初試准考證號碼後 5 碼）＿＿.

一、朗讀短文

請先利用 1 分鐘的時間閱讀下面的短文，然後在 2 分鐘內以正常的
速度，清楚正確的朗讀下面的短文。

A recent study maintains that second-hand cigarette
smoke does more harm to nonsmokers than to smokers.
While cigarette smokers' bodies have adapted to the
adverse effects of smoking, nonsmokers do not have
this "benefit," so they are much more affected by smoke
in their environment.

＊　　　　＊　　　　＊

Mail can be delivered faster if the correct zip code
is part of the address. The letters ZIP stand for Zone
Improvement Planning. Every address in the United
States has a zip code of five numbers. Each number
has a meaning. The United States Postal Service has
divided the country into ten large parts. A number
between 0 and 9 has been given to each part. The first

number of any zip code informs postal workers of the large part of the country to which the letter or package goes. The second and third numbers refer to the sections within the large area. The last two numbers stand for the local post office to which the mail goes. Can you see why everyone should use zip codes on mail?

二、回答問題

這個部分共有 10 題。題目已事先錄音，每題經由耳機播出二次，不印在試題冊上。第 1 至 5 題，每題回答時間 15 秒；第 6 至 10 題，每題回答時間 30 秒。每題播出後，請立即回答。回答時，不一定要用完整的句子，但請在作答時間內儘量的表達。

三、看圖敘述

下面有一張圖片及四個相關的問題,請在 1 分半鐘內完成作答。
作答時,請直接回答,不需將題號及題目唸出。首先請利用 30 秒
的時間看圖及問題。

1. 這是什麼地方?
2. 這裡的擺設如何?
3. 圖裡的人在做什麼?
4. 如果還有時間,請詳細敘述圖片中的人、事、物。

*請將下列自我介紹的句子再唸一遍,請開始:

My seat number is ___(複試座位號碼後 5 碼)___, and my
registration number is ___(初試准考證號碼後 5 碼)___.

寫作口說能力測驗 ⑧ 詳解

寫作能力測驗詳解

一、中譯英（40分）

昨天我在超級市場買東西的時候，遇見了我的國中同學瑪麗（Mary）。我們已經有十年沒見了。她看起來跟以前完全不同。她比以前瘦多了。我們一起去咖啡館坐了一會。畢竟我們很久沒見了。

When I was shopping at the supermarket yesterday, I ran into my junior high school classmate, Mary. We have not seen each other for ten years. She looks totally different from before. She is much thinner now. We went to a coffee shop together for a while. After all, we had not seen each other for a long time.

【註】supermarket ('supɚ,mɑrkɪt) n. 超級市場
  run into 偶然遇到 (= *bump into* = *come across*)
  totally ('totḷɪ) *adv.* 完全地
  thin (θɪn) *adj.* 瘦的
  for a while 一會兒 ***after all*** 畢竟

二、**英文作文**（60分）

【作文範例】

September 30th, 2008

To whom it may concern,

　　I was contacted by your company recently for an interview. I was scheduled to be at your company at three o'clock in the afternoon next Wednesday. I am very grateful that I was given the opportunity for an interview with your company. However, something has come up unexpectedly, and I am required to be present at a different location at that time.

　　I have every intention to interview with your company, however, this newly developed situation is of importance and I must be present. I would like to request a postponement of my appointment until next Thursday, or any other time that is convenient for you, if possible. I sincerely hope that this change of schedule won't cause you any undue inconvenience. I am truly sorry to have to make this request and I am really looking forward to interviewing with your fine organization.

　　Please take this matter into consideration. Thank you very much.

Sincerely yours,
Wendy

【註】 contact ('kɑntækt) v. 聯繫

recently ('risntlı) adv. 最近

interview ('ıntə,vju) n. v. 面試

schedule ('skɛdʒul) v. 排定

grateful ('gretfəl) adj. 感激的

opportunity (,ɑpə'tjunətı) n. 機會

come up 發生

unexpectedly (,ʌnık'spɛktıdlı) adv. 意外地；突然

require (rı'kwaır) v. 需要

present ('prɛzənt) adj. 出席的；在場的

location (lo'keʃən) n. 地點；地方

intention (ın'tɛnʃən) n. 意念；打算

newly ('njulı) adv. 新近；最近

situation (sıtʃu'eʃən) n. 情況

of importance 重要的 (= *important*)

request (rı'kwɛst) v. n. 要求

postponement (post'ponmənt) n. 延期

sincerely (sın'sırlı) adv. 誠懇地

undue (ʌn'dju) adj. 不應有的

look forward to V-ing 期待

organization (,ɔrgənaı'zeʃən) n. 組織；機構

matter ('mætə) n. 問題

consideration (kən,sıdə'reʃən) n. 考慮

take sth. into consideration 考慮某事

口說能力測驗詳解

＊請在 15 秒內完成並唸出下列自我介紹的句子，請開始：

My seat number is ＿＿＿（複試座位號碼後 5 碼）＿＿＿, and my
registration number is ＿＿＿（初試准考證號碼後 5 碼）＿＿＿.

一、朗讀短文

請先利用 1 分鐘的時間閱讀下面的短文，然後在 2 分鐘內以正常的速度，
清楚正確的朗讀下面的短文。

A recent study maintains that second-hand cigarette
smoke does more harm to nonsmokers than to smokers.
While cigarette smokers' bodies have adapted to the
adverse effects of smoking, nonsmokers do not have this
"benefit," so they are much more affected by smoke in
their environment.

最近的研究強調，二手煙對非吸煙者所造成的傷害比吸煙
者來得大。由於吸煙者的身體已經能適應抽煙的不良影響，而非
吸煙者卻沒有這項「利益」，所以他們更容易被其周圍的煙所影
響。

【註】maintain〔 men'ten 〕v. 主張；強調
　　　second-hand〔'sɛkənd'hænd 〕adj. 二手的
　　　cigarette〔'sɪgə,rɛt 〕n. 香煙
　　　do harm to 對～有害　　　adapt〔 ə'dæpt 〕v. 適應
　　　adverse〔 əd'vɜs 〕adj. 不利的
　　　effect〔 ɪ'fɛkt 〕n. 影響
　　　benefit〔'bɛnəfɪt 〕n. 利益　　　affect〔 ə'fɛkt 〕v. 影響

Mail can be delivered faster if the correct zip code is part of the address. The letters ZIP stand for Zone Improvement Planning. Every address in the United States has a zip code of five numbers. Each number has a meaning. The United States Postal Service has divided the country into ten large parts. A number between 0 and 9 has been given to each part. The first number of any zip code informs postal workers of the large part of the country to which the letter or package goes. The second and third numbers refer to the sections within the large area. The last two numbers stand for the local post office to which the mail goes. Can you see why everyone should use zip codes on mail?

如果地址中寫有正確的郵遞區號，信就可以送得比較快。ZIP 這個字代表「區域改善計劃」。美國的每個地址，都有含五位數的郵遞區號，每個號碼都有其意義。「美國郵政局」將全國分為十大區域。每個區域分配一個 0 到 9 之間的數字。郵遞區號的第一個數字，可以告訴郵政人員，這個信件或包裹是寄往哪一區。第二及第三個數字是指大區域中的小區域。最後兩個數字，代表信件所要寄到的當地郵局。你知道為什麼每個人都要在信件上填寫郵遞區號了嗎？

【註】 mail (mel) *n.* 信件　　deliver (dɪˈlɪvɚ) *v.* 遞送
zip code 郵遞區號　　address (əˈdrɛs) *n.* 地址
letter (ˈlɛtɚ) *n.* 字母　　*stand for* 代表
zone (zon) *n.* 區域　　improvement (ɪmˈpruvmənt) *n.* 改良
postal (ˈpostl̩) *adj.* 郵政的　　divide (dəˈvaɪd) *v.* 區分
inform (ɪnˈfɔrm) *v.* 通知　　package (ˈpækɪdʒ) *n.* 包裹
refer to 是指　　section (ˈsɛkʃən) *n.* 區域
local (ˈlokl̩) *adj.* 當地的

二、回答問題

這個部分共有 10 題。題目已事先錄音，每題經由耳機播出二次，不印在試題冊上。第 1 至 5 題，每題回答時間 15 秒；第 6 至 10 題，每題回答時間 30 秒。每題播出後，請立即回答。回答時，不一定要用完整的句子，但請在作答時間內儘量的表達。

※ 第 1 至第 5 題，每題回答時間 15 秒。

1. Q ： What is your favorite sport? Why?

　　你最喜歡的運動是什麼？為什麼？

A1 ： My favorite sport would be baseball. I don't really know how to play baseball, but I sure do enjoy watching it. It is especially exciting when the team you are cheering for makes a home run.

　　我最喜歡的運動是棒球。我不是很會打棒球，可是我很喜歡看棒球賽。當你支持的球隊打出全壘打時，特別令人興奮。

A2 ： My favorite sport is basketball. I especially like to watch NBA games. Those NBA players are amazing. It seems like they can all fly through the air with ease.

　　我最喜歡的運動是籃球。我特別喜歡看 NBA 球賽。那些 NBA 球員們真神奇。他們好像都能很輕易地在空中飛翔。

【註】　1. cheer〔tʃɪr〕v. 歡呼；為～加油
　　　　home run 全壘打
　　　　amazing〔ə'mezɪŋ〕adj. 神奇的
　　　　with ease 輕易地（= *easily*）

2. Q : What do you usually do on weekends? Why?

　　　 你週末通常都做些什麼？為什麼？

A1 : I don't like to go out much, so I spend most of my weekends sitting around home watching TV. When I do go out, I only buy food and come home to eat.

　　　 我不太喜歡出去，所以在週末時，我大多無所事事，待在家裡看電視。我要是真的出去，都只是為了要買食物回家吃。

A2 : I like to go out with my friends and have fun on weekends. We usually go shopping or to the movies. Sometimes we will go to the KTV to sing. That way, my weekend is fun and fulfilling.

　　　 我喜歡在週末和朋友出去玩。我們通常會去逛街，或去看電影。有時候我們會去 KTV 唱歌。那樣子，我的週末就會又好玩又充實。

A3 : I almost always have to work on weekends, which makes going out to have fun not possible. I would like to go out on weekends but I am really strapped for money so I have to work as much as I can.

　　　 我幾乎週末都要上班，所以我不太可能出去玩。我其實很想在週末出去玩，可是我很需要錢，所以我要儘量多上一點班。

【註】 2. *sit around*　無所事事

　　　 fulfilling (fulˈfɪlɪŋ) *adj.* 令人滿意的；充實的

　　　 strap (stræp) *v.* 約束；束縛

3. Q ： What is the place you would like to go most? Why?

你最想去的地方是哪裡？為什麼？

A1 ： I would like to visit Disneyland. It is the land of happiness. Also it is every child's dream to visit Disneyland.

我想去迪士尼樂園。那裡是快樂的國度。而且去迪士尼樂園是每個小孩的夢想。

A2 ： I have always wanted to visit San Francisco. I heard it is the most romantic city in America. I would like to ride the cable cars up and down the hills and see the Golden Gate Bridge. If I get to go, I will die a happy man.

我一直都想去舊金山。我聽說它是美國最浪漫的城市。我想要搭纜車上下山，還要去看金門大橋。如果我能去的話，我就死而無憾了。

4. Q ： What time do you usually go to bed at night? Why do you go to bed at that particular time?

你晚上通常幾點睡覺？為什麼會在那個時間去睡覺？

【註】　3. Disneyland ('dɪznɪ,lænd) *n.* 迪士尼樂園
land (lænd) *n.* 國度
romantic (ro'mæntɪk) *adj.* 浪漫的
ride (raɪd) *v.* 搭乘　　***cable car*** 纜車
up and down 上下地　　***die happy*** 死而無憾
　4. particular (pə'tɪkjələ) *adj.* 特定的

A1 : I usually go to bed at about one o'clock in the morning. My favorite TV show comes on at midnight. I can't go to sleep without watching it.

> 我通常在凌晨一點才去睡覺。我最喜歡的電視節目在十二點開始。要是沒看到那個節目，我會睡不著覺。

A2 : I go to bed early so I can get up early. Sleeping late is just not healthy. You know what they say, "The early bird catches the worm." With enough sleep, I can have lots of energy in the morning to do what I have to do.

> 我會早睡，這樣我才能早起。晚睡實在是不健康。大家都說：「早起的鳥兒有蟲吃。」有充足的睡眠，我早上才會很有精神去做我該做的事。

---

5. Q : Do you like to eat hamburgers? Why?

> 你喜歡吃漢堡嗎？為什麼？

A1 : I love hamburgers. They are the most tasty and convenient food available. I especially like those large flame broiled hamburgers with bacon and cheese. Just give me one of those and I'll be a happy camper.

> 我很喜歡吃漢堡。那是最美味，而且又最方便的食物。我特別喜歡吃那種有培根和起司的火烤大漢堡。只要給我一個，我就會很開心了。

【註】 4. ***come on*** 開始　midnight (ˈmɪdˌnaɪt) *n.* 半夜
　　　 sleep late 晚睡　energy (ˈɛnɚdʒɪ) *n.* 活力
　　 5. tasty (ˈtestɪ) *adj.* 美味的　flame (flem) *n.* 火焰
　　　 broil (brɔɪl) *v.* 烤　bacon (ˈbekən) *n.* 培根
　　　 a happy camper 開心的人

A2 : How can anybody eat hamburgers? They are the worst food ever invented by mankind. People don't call it junk food for no reason. Hamburgers are greasy and are made from the worst meat available. Besides, I am a vegetarian anyway.

怎麼會有人去吃漢堡？那是人類所發明最糟糕的一種食物。大家叫它垃圾食物，不是沒理由的。漢堡很油膩，並且是用最爛的肉所做成的。而且，反正我吃素。

※ 第 6 至第 10 題，每題回答時間 30 秒。

6. Q ： Did you watch TV last night? What program did you watch? Why?

你昨晚有沒有看電視？你看了哪一個節目？為什麼？

A1 : I didn't watch TV last night. It's not because I don't want to watch TV, it's because I don't have a TV at home.

我昨晚沒有看電視。不是因為我不想看，而是我家裡沒電視。

【註】　5. invent〔ɪn'vɛnt〕v. 發明
mankind〔‚mæn'kaɪnd〕n. 人類
junk〔dʒʌŋk〕n. 垃圾　***junk food*** 垃圾食物
greasy〔'grizɪ〕adj. 油膩的
vegetarian〔‚vɛdʒə'tɛrɪən〕n. 素食者

A2 : I watched some silly variety show last night featuring the famous show host, Jacky Wu. It was such a dumb show that I don't even remember what it was about. I just kind of stumbled upon it accidentally.

> 我昨晚看了由名節目主持人吳宗憲，所主持的一個愚蠢的綜藝節目。那個節目實在是太白癡了，我根本記不起來演的是什麼。我只是不小心看到的。

---

7. Q : Will you cook dinner for your family tonight? Why or why not?

> 你今晚會不會為你的家人做晚餐？為什麼會，或為什麼不會？

A1 : Of course I will. I love cooking and I love to see people devour my creations greedily. It gives me a great sense of achievement. Also I would like to think of myself as a pretty good cook.

> 我當然會囉。我很喜歡烹飪，並且我喜歡看大家貪婪地吞食我的傑作。那樣會使我很有成就感。而且我自認是個蠻不錯的廚師。

【註】 6. *variety show* 綜藝節目
　　　 host (host) *n.* 電視節目主持人
　　　 feature (ˈfitʃɚ) *v.* 以～為特色
　　　 dumb (dʌm) *adj.* 愚蠢的　　*kind of* 有一點
　　　 stumble (ˈstʌmbḷ) *v.* 偶然發現
　　　 accidentally (ˌæksəˈdɛntḷɪ) *adv.* 偶然地

　　 7. devour (dɪˈvaʊr) *v.* 狼吞虎嚥
　　　 creation (krɪˈeʃən) *n.* 創作
　　　 greedily (ˈgridəlɪ) *adv.* 貪婪地
　　　 achievement (əˈtʃivmənt) *n.* 成就　　cook (kʊk) *n.* 廚師

A2： Well, I don't think that I will cook for my family tonight. First of all, I don't know how to cook and I really don't think that anyone would be crazy enough to eat my cooking. Secondly, we have a maid at home and she is a very good cook. So we don't have to worry about not having people to cook dinner for my family.

> 嗯，我不認為我今天晚上會為我的家人做晚餐。第一，我不會做，而且，我覺得不會有人瘋狂到想要吃我煮的菜。第二，我們家裡有女佣，她菜做得不錯。所以我們不必擔心沒人做晚餐給我們吃。

8. Q ： You have a toothache, what will you say to your dentist when you go see him?

> 你的牙在痛，你去看牙醫的時候，你會跟他說什麼？

A1： Ouch! My tooth is killing me. You need to hurry up and do something. I don't know where it hurts but it is driving me insane.

> 哎喲！我的牙痛死了。你要快點來幫幫我。我不知道哪裡痛，可是卻痛得我快發瘋了。

【註】 7. maid〔med〕*n.* 女佣
8. toothache〔'tuθ,ek〕*n.* 牙痛
dentist〔'dɛntɪst〕*n.* 牙醫　　kill〔kɪl〕*v.* 使痛苦
do something 想辦法　　drive〔draɪv〕*v.* 迫使
ouch〔autʃ〕*interj.* 哎喲
insane〔ɪn'sen〕*adj.* 瘋狂的（= *crazy*）

A2 : It is a very sharp pain. It hurts when I use it to chew on food. It also hurts when I eat or drink cold stuff. I can't eat because of this miserable tooth.

那是一種劇烈的疼痛。當我用它來咀嚼食物時就會痛。當我吃或喝冷的東西也會痛。因為這顆討厭的牙齒，我都不能吃東西。

---

9. Q : What kind of transportation do you most often utilize? Why? 你最常使用的交通工具是什麼？為什麼？

A1 : I use the MRT the most. I live right by an MRT station and I ride it to work all the time. It is really convenient and cheap.

我最常坐捷運。我就住在捷運站附近，而且我都坐捷運去上班。真是既方便又便宜。

A2 : I ride my motor scooter everywhere I go. It is fast and agile. I can weave in and out of traffic with ease. Although it is not safe to do so, the convenience it brings me is unmatchable.

我不管去哪裡都騎摩托車。既方便又靈活。我能很輕易地在車陣中鑽來鑽去。雖然那樣做不安全，但是所帶來的便利，實在是什麼都比不上。

【註】 8. sharp〔ʃɑrp〕*adj.* 劇烈的　　chew〔tʃu〕*v.* 咀嚼
stuff〔stʌf〕*n.* 東西
miserable〔'mɪzərəbḷ〕*adj.* 惱人的

9. transportation〔ˌtrænspɚ'teʃən〕*n.* 交通工具
utilize〔'jutḷˌaɪz〕*v.* 利用　　agile〔'ædʒaɪl〕*adj.* 靈活的
weave〔wiv〕*v.* 迂迴行進；做閃避動作
with ease 輕易地
unmatchable〔ʌn'mætʃəbḷ〕*adj.* 不能相比的

10. Q : If you go to the zoo, what animal would you like
to see most? Why?

如果你去動物園，你會最想看哪種動物？為什麼？

A1 : I definitely want to see the koala bears, Patrick and
Harley. I think they are the cutest things on earth.
Too bad we can only see them from a distance. I
would really like to hold them.

我絕對要去看無尾熊，派克與哈雷。我認為牠們是全世界最
可愛的東西。真可惜我們只能從遠處看牠們。我真的很想抱
抱牠們。

A2 : I think I would want to see the apes. I want to
observe their living habits. These animals are highly
intelligent and know how to use simple tools. I
think it would be really interesting. After all, they
are our ancestors.

我覺得我會想去看猿猴。我想要觀察牠們的生活習性。這些
動物非常聰明，而且會使用簡單的工具。我認為那會很有趣。
畢竟，牠們是我們的祖先。

【註】　10. definitely (ˈdɛfənɪtlɪ) adv. 一定；當然
　　　　　koala (kəˈɑlə) n. 無尾熊　　　cute (kjut) adj. 可愛的
　　　　　distance (ˈdɪstəns) n. 距離　　　ape (ep) n. 猿猴
　　　　　observe (əbˈzɜv) v. 觀察
　　　　　highly (ˈhaɪlɪ) adv. 非常地
　　　　　intelligent (ɪnˈtɛlədʒənt) adj. 聰明的
　　　　　tool (tul) n. 工具　　　*after all* 畢竟
　　　　　ancestor (ˈænsɛstə) n. 祖先

三、看圖敘述

下面有一張圖片及四個相關的問題，請在 1 分半鐘內完成作答。作答時，請直接回答，不需將題號及題目唸出。首先請利用 30 秒的時間看圖及問題。

1. 這是什麼地方？

This is a classroom.

這是一間教室。

2. 這裡的擺設如何？

These chairs are arranged in perfect order. The wall is clean with nothing on it. The decoration is quite simple.

椅子排列得非常整齊。牆壁很乾淨，上面沒有任何東西。這裡的擺設很簡單。

3. 圖裡的人在做什麼？

The girl in the front is resting her chin on her hand. The girl behind her is looking forward. The second girl to the left is olding a pen. The first girl to the left is unpacking her bag.

前面的女孩用手托住她的下巴。坐在她後面的女孩正看著前面。左邊第二個女孩握著一支筆。左邊第一個女孩正打開她的包包拿東西。

【註】 2. arrange〔ə'rendʒ〕v. 排列　　***in order*** 整齊的
decoration〔͵dɛkə'reʃən〕n. 裝飾
　　　3. rest〔rɛst〕v. 倚靠　　chin〔tʃɪn〕n. 下巴
look forward 向前看
unpack〔ʌn'pæk〕v. 打開取物

4. 如果還有時間，請詳細敘述圖片中的人、事、物。

During the break, students are chatting with their teacher and other classmates. The girl with glasses is sort of tired, so she is resting her chin on her hand. The girl in overalls is listening carefully to what the teacher is saying. The second girl to the left is trying to write down some notes. The first girl to the left just bought a bottle of soda. She is putting her wallet back into the bag.

下課的時候，同學們都在和老師，以及其他同學聊天。戴眼鏡的女孩有點累了，所以她用手托住下巴。穿吊帶褲的女孩，仔細在聽老師說話。左邊第二個女孩正試著要做些筆記。左邊第一個女孩剛買了一瓶汽水。她正要把她的皮夾放回袋子裡。

【註】 4. break (brek) n. 下課時間
chat (tʃæt) v. 聊天的
glasses (ˈglæsɪz) n. pl. 眼鏡
sort of 有一點　　overalls (ˈovɚˌɔlz) n. pl. 吊帶褲
note (not) n. 筆記　　soda (ˈsodə) n. 汽水
wallet (ˈwɑlɪt) n. 皮包

＊請將下列自我介紹的句子再唸一遍，請開始：

My seat number is ＿＿(複試座位號碼後5碼)＿＿, and my registration number is ＿＿(初試准考證號碼後5碼)＿＿.

ITTC 財團法人 語言訓練測驗中心
全民英語能力分級檢定測驗成績單
General English Proficiency Test Examinee's Score Record

測驗日期 Test Date	: 2008/03/29	姓　名 Name	：劉怡玲 LIU.YI-LING
級　數 Level	：中級 Intermediate	身分證件字號 ID	：F227598351
准考證號碼 Reg. No	：422-01-16928	出生年月日 Date of Birth	：1992/10/01

聽力 Listening	閱讀 Reading	寫作 Writing	口說 Speaking	達複試通過標準。
112	99	84	90	

說　明

1. 「全民英語能力分級檢定測驗」係教育部核准財團法人語言訓練測驗中心辦理。
2. 通過標準：

級數	初試				複試		
	測驗項目	通過標準	各項滿分		測驗項目	通過標準	各項滿分
高級	聽力/閱讀能力測驗	兩項測驗成績總合達160分,且其中任一項成績不低於72分。	120分		寫作/口說能力測驗	3級分	5級分
中高級 中級					寫作/口說能力測驗	80分	100分
初級					寫作能力測驗 口說能力測驗	70分 80分	100分

3. 初試成績通過者,得參加該級數同梯次或接連下一梯次之複試;如兩次複試未報考、或報考但未出席、或出席但未通過者須重新報考初試;惟一旦通過同梯次複試,即不得再報考下一梯次複試(詳見97年報名手冊第7頁)。
4. 擬申請成績複查者,請於成績公布日起十天內申請(以郵戳為憑),逾期申請恕不受理(詳見97年報名手冊第24頁)。
5. 初、複試皆通過者,發給合格證書(成績單及合格證書一併寄發);已取得合格證書者,一年內不得再報考同級數或較低級數之測驗。

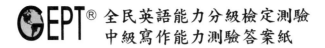

座位號碼：＿＿＿＿＿＿＿＿＿＿＿　　　試卷別：＿＿＿＿＿＿

第一部分請由第1行開始作答，請勿隔行書寫。

_____

_____

_____

_____

_____

_____

_____

_____

_____

_____

_____

_____

_____

_____

_____

_____

_____

_____

_____

_____

_____

_____

_____

25

30

35

40

附錄

全民英語能力分級檢定測驗簡介

　　「全民英語能力分級檢定測驗」(General English Proficiency Test)，簡稱「全民英檢」（GEPT ），旨在提供我國各階段英語學習者一套公平、有效且可靠之英語能力評量工具，測驗對象包括在校學生及一般社會人士，可做為學習成果檢定、教學改進及公民營機構甄選人才等之參考。

　　本測驗為標準參照測驗（criterion-referenced test ），參考我國英語教育體制，制定分級標準，整套系統共分五級──初級（Elementary ）、中級（Intermediate ）、中高級（High-Intermediate ）、高級（Advanced ）、優級（Superior ）。每級訂有明確能力標準，報考者可依英語能力選擇適當級數報考，每級均包含聽、說、讀、寫四項完整的測驗，通過所報考級數的能力標準即可取得該級的合格證書。

中級英語能力測驗簡介

I. 通過中級檢定者的英語能力

聽	讀	寫	說
在日常生活情境中，能聽懂一般的會話；能大致聽懂公共場所廣播、氣象報告及廣告等。在工作情境中，能聽懂簡易的產品介紹與操作說明。能大致聽懂外籍人士的談話及詢問。	在日常生活情境中，能閱讀短文、故事、私人信件、廣告、傳單、簡介及使用說明等。在工作情境中，能閱讀工作須知、公告、操作手冊、例行的文件、傳真、電報等。	能寫簡單的書信、故事及心得等。對於熟悉且與個人經歷相關的主題，能以簡易的文字表達。	在日常生活情境中，能以簡易英語交談或描述一般事物，能介紹自己的生活作息、工作、家庭、經歷等，並可對一般話題陳述看法。在工作情境中，能進行簡單的答詢，並與外籍人士交談溝通。

II. 測驗項目

	初　　試		複　　試	
測驗項目	聽力測驗	閱讀能力測驗	寫作能力測驗	口說能力測驗
總題數	45 題	40 題	2 題	13~14 題
作答時間	約 30 分鐘	45 分鐘	40 分鐘	約 15 分鐘
測驗內容	看圖辨義 問答 簡短對話	詞彙和結構 段落填空 閱讀理解	中譯英 英文作文	朗讀短文 回答問題 看圖敘述
總測驗時間 （含試前、 試後說明）	兩項一共約需 2 小時		約需 1 小時	約需 1 小時

　　聽力及閱讀能力測驗成績採標準計分方式，滿分 120 分。寫作及口說能力測驗成績採整體式評分，使用級分制，分為0～5級分，再轉換成百分制。各項成績通過標準如下：

III. 成績計算及通過標準

初試	通過標準	滿分	複試	通過標準	滿分
聽力測驗 閱讀能力測驗	兩項測驗成績總和達160分，且其中任一項成績不低於 72 分。（自 97 年起生效，不溯及既往）	120 120	寫作能力測驗 口說能力測驗	80 80	100 100

Ⅳ. 寫作能力測驗級分說明

第一部份：中譯英

級　分	分　數	説　　　　明
5	40	內容能充分表達題意，文段 (text) 結構及連貫性甚佳。用字遣詞、文法、拼字、標點及大小寫幾乎無誤。
4	32	內容適切表達題意，句子結構及連貫性大致良好。用字遣詞、文法、拼字、標點及大小寫偶有錯誤，但不妨礙題意之表達。
3	34	內容未能完全表達題意，句子結構鬆散，連貫性不足。用字遣詞及文法有誤，但不妨礙題意之表達，且拼字、標點及大小寫也有錯誤。
2	16	僅能局部表達原文題意，句子結構不良、有誤，且大多難以理解並缺乏連貫性。字彙有限，文法、拼字、標點及大小寫有許多錯誤。
1	8	內容無法表達題意，語句沒有結構概念及連貫性，無法理解。字彙極有限，文法、拼字、標點及大小寫之錯誤多且嚴重。
0	0	未答/等同未答。

第二部份：英文作文

級　分	分　數	説　　　　明
5	60	內容適切表達題目要求，組織甚佳，靈活運用字彙及句型，句型有變化，文法、拼字或標點符號無重大錯誤。
4	48	內容符合題目要求，組織大致良好，正確運用字彙及句型，文法、拼字或標點符號鮮有重大錯誤。
3	36	內容大致符合題目要求，但未完全達意，組織尚可，能夠運用的字彙有限，文法、拼字、標點符號有誤。
2	24	內容未能符合題目要求，大多難以理解，組織不良，能夠運用的字彙有限，文法、拼字、標點符號有許多錯誤。
1	12	內容未能符合題目要求，完全無法理解，沒有組織，能夠運用的字彙有限，文法、拼字、標點符號有過多錯誤。
0	0	未答/等同未答。

V. 口說能力測驗級分說明

級　分	分　數	說　　　　　明
5	100	發音清晰、正確，語調正確、自然；對應內容切題，表達流暢；語法、字彙使用自如，雖仍偶有錯誤，但無礙溝通。
4	80	發音大致清晰、正確，語調大致正確、自然；對應內容切題，語法、字彙之使用雖有錯誤，但無礙溝通。
3	60	發音、語調時有錯誤，因而影響聽者對其語意的瞭解。已能掌握基本句型結構，語法仍有錯誤；且因字彙、片語有限，阻礙表達。
2	40	發音、語調錯誤均多，朗讀時常因缺乏辨識能力而略過不讀；因語法、字彙常有錯誤，而無法進行有效的溝通。
1	20	發音、語調錯誤多且嚴重，又因語法錯誤甚多，認識之單字片語有限，無法清楚表達，幾乎無溝通能力。
0	0	未答/等同未答。

　　凡應考且合乎規定者，無論成績通過與否一律發給成績單。初試及複試皆通過者，發給合格證書。成績紀錄自測驗日期起由本中心保存 2 年。

　　初試通過者，可於一年內單獨報考複試，得重複報考。惟複試一旦通過，即不得再報考。

　　已通過本英檢測驗某一級數並取得合格證書者，自複試測驗日期起 1 年內不得再報考同級數或較低級數之測驗。違反本規定報考者，其應試資格將被取消。

（以上資料取自「全民英檢學習網站」http://www.gept.org.tw）

劉毅英文家教班成績優異同學獎學金排行榜

姓　名	學　校	總金額	姓　名	學　校	總金額	姓　名	學　校	總金額	姓　名	學　校	總金額
蕭煥祁	成功高中	174350	陳彥同	建國中學	41266	賴映君	靜修女中	26900	許瑋峻	延平高中	21700
江冠廷	建國中學	162200	林鈺恆	中和高中	39800	王文洲	建國中學	26500	王宣鈞	延平高中	21500
陳柏瑞	建國中學	158600	陳瑞邦	成功高中	38400	賴奕丞	明倫高中	26500	林育如	大同高中	21400
羅培瑞	延平高中	148600	賴鈺錡	明倫高中	37650	李昕	育成高中	25900	李承芳	中山女中	21400
翁御修	師大附中	138500	林敬傑	成功高中	36800	江咸君	金陵女中	25800	歐陽嘉爾	建國中學	21375
王泓琦	中山女中	135200	鄭翔仁	師大附中	36650	許曄芥	百齡高中	25800	林雨潔	中山女中	21300
楊蕙寧	中崙高中	133000	塗皓宇	建國中學	36634	張政榕	三民高中	25500	王子豪	師大附中	21300
潘貞諭	北一女中	132800	蘇郁涵	大理高中	36300	何宇屏	陽明高中	25500	王楚璿	北一女中	21266
薛宜婷	北一女中	131300	溫育菱	景美女中	35400	練子立	海山高中	25400	徐永安	建國中學	21200
簡翔凌	北一女中	129500	林芮年	北一女中	34900	施恩潔	北一女中	25300	張逸軒	建國中學	21000
王冠宇	建國中學	122700	楊玄詳	明志國中	34200	吳宇晴	中山女中	25200	朱祐霆	成淵高中	21000
張寧珊	北一女中	120600	陳柏瑋	建國中學	33900	許顥升	內湖高中	25100	賴俊銘	成功高中	20800
林則方	明倫高中	120400	陳冠勳	中正高中	33700	李國維	建國中學	25000	謝昀彤	建國中學	20767
呂育昇	建國中學	120300	李祖茶	新店高中	33400	林大鈞	建國中學	24900	何翌穗	北一女中	20666
邵祺皓	建國中學	119100	李洋	師大附中	33300	高昀婕	北一女中	24800	陳冠芸	華江高中	20600
葉書偉	師大附中	116600	徐子瑜	內湖高中	32900	劉桐	北一女中	24800	劉詩瑜	中崙高中	20500
蘇聖博	建國中學	110600	廖家呈	師大附中	32700	黃愨鈞	建國中學	24600	劉奕廷	北一女中	20500
沈奕均	北一女中	109000	李宗鴻	成功高中	32500	鄭惟仁	建國中學	24500	羅偉恩	師大附中	20500
洪培裕	成功高中	108300	王俊智	大直高中	32400	邵世儒	成功高中	24400	黃雅晨	中和高中	20400
陳允禛	格致高中	108000	洪辰宗	師大附中	31800	許瑞云	中山女中	24350	賴科維	延平高中	20300
曾文勤	北一女中	107400	陳姵懿	永春高中	31700	陳奕仲	建國中學	24300	董芸	松山高中	20300
吳玨珬	中崙高中	104100	黃珮瑄	中山女中	31450	高立蘅	板橋高中	24300	張延寧	明倫高中	20300
蔣耀樟	師大附中	102500	楊竣翔	建國高中	31200	吳孟宥	成淵高中	24100	高聖峰	建國中學	20200
林泳亨	薇閣國小	99000	邵偉桓	大直高中	30950	楊肇焓	建國中學	24100	阮柏劭	華江高中	20200
陳宇甫	北一女中	94900	王宣期	中山女中	30700	黃安正	松山高中	24100	郭芊妤	文德女中	20100
林渝軒	建國中學	81401	紀乃慈	衛理女中	30600	高煒哲	成功高中	23800	黎上瑋	麗山高中	20100
蔡景勾	內湖高中	68300	許益誠	成功高中	30600	林俐吟	中山女中	23750	徐子洋	延平高中	20100
曾昱誠	建國中學	63200	吳則緯	成功高中	29600	陳昇佶	華江高中	23400	樊瑞	建國中學	20100
李家偉	成功高中	60800	陳邦尹	成功高中	29500	張孟年	北一女中	23200	王柏凱	建國中學	20100
莊子豎	蘭園中部	58700	吳其慶	延平高中	29300	陳冠綸	成功高中	23100	車庭玄	大理高中	19900
鄭婷云	師大附中	58200	劉彥廷	成功高中	29200	郭清怡	師大附中	23100	吳姿菁	北一女中	19850
丁哲浩	建國中學	58200	邱逸雯	縣三重高中	29100	李孟蘋	景美女中	23000	蔡竺君	中山女中	19600
薛羽彤	北一女中	57468	詹其穎	板橋高中	29000	郯蕙綸	板橋高中	23000	陳藝帆	南山高中	19600
謝伊妍	北一女中	53400	高行熲	西松高中	29000	邱容宇	師大附中	22950	卓晉宇	華江高中	19600
蔡書旻	格致高中	52400	魏雲杰	成功高中	28800	羅婷庭	成功高中	22800	吳承恩	成功高中	19500
白子洋	建國中學	51800	邱柏盛	進修生	28700	張景翔	師大附中	22700	許珩維	大直高中	19400
陳光炫	建國中學	51500	姜德婷	延平高中	28700	許晏魁	竹林國中	22650	顏葳澤	華江高中	19400
陳亭熹	北一女中	50400	劉仁偉	板橋高中	28600	陳明	建國中學	22650	劉彥甫	南湖高中	19300
徐大鈞	建國中學	49500	張薇貞	景美女中	28600	陳韶安	進修生	22600	陳育廷	板橋高中	19300
朱庭萱	北一女中	48317	謝孟哲	延平高中	28500	梁耕瑋	建國中學	22600	劉家伶	成功高中	19300
顏汝翊	北一女中	48100	陳琳涵	成功高中	28250	曾煜凱	成淵高中	22400	許瑋宸	建國中學	19250
林立	建國中學	46575	蘇佳瑜	松山高中	28200	洪詩涵	中和高中	22400	趙于萱	中正高中	19200
劉宜陵	中崙高中	45600	蘇傳堯	師大附中	28100	賴明楨	松山高中	22400	陳昇愷	建國中學	19175
呂宗倫	南湖高中	44850	辛亞潔	大同高中	27900	魏宏旻	中和高中	22300	蕭允祈	東山高中	19150
張立昀	北一女中	44667	劉玠均	北一女中	27700	黃韻帆	板橋高中	22300	曹瑞哲	成功高中	19100
許四融	建國中學	44600	蔡佳伶	麗山高中	27500	范綱晉	成功高中	22200	楊其儒	師大附中	18900
蔡佳君	北一女中	44300	鄭昌哽	大同高中	27500	董豐儀	育成高中	22100	陳宜琳	北一女中	18800
林琬姍	北一女中	44283	楊博閎	海山高中	27450	鄭凱文	建國中學	22000	曹臆醒	內湖高中	18800
陳瑋欣	北一女中	44200	林俊瑋	建國高中	27400	姜思羽	中山女中	22000	吳冠宏	建國中學	18700
林臻	北一女中	42700	朱哲毅	師大附中	27400	柯鈞崴	成淵高中	21900	張博勛	建國中學	18700
張瀚陽	中正高中	41900	黃堂榮	延平高中	27100	郭貞里	北一女中	21850	李紘賢	板橋高中	18700
呂學宸	師大附中	41300	吳怡萱	永春高中	27100	曾泓祥	建國中學	21800	柯穎瑄	北一女中	18700

姓名	學校	總金額
陳嘉敏	北一女中	18600
李芷涵	中山女中	18600
郭偵丈	中山女中	18600
林懿葶	中山女中	18575
呂柔霏	松山高中	18550
吳定軒	板橋高中	18400
黃瀞儀	樹林高中	18400
張智堯	建國中學	18300
林詩涵	南湖高中	18300
蕭樂山	建國中學	18000
許至禎	明倫高中	18000
李心蕙	海山高中	17800
柯文斌	明倫高中	17700
龔　毅	師大附中	17700
洪健雄	成功高中	17600
張育銓	成功高中	17600
左如元	育成高中	17600
姚政徽	景美女中	17500
李芃霓	華僑高中	17500
賴又華	北一女中	17400
王沛安	景美女中	17300
陳胤禎	成功高中	17300
位芷甄	北一女中	17250
許佳雯	板橋高中	17200
吳元魁	建國中學	17200
江昱嫺	北一女中	17000
陳冠宇	明倫高中	17000
林士傑	建國中學	17000
李明叡	建國中學	17000
吳語潔	南山高中	16900
簡上祐	成淵高中	16800
蔡柏晏	北一女中	16800
周佳妮	重考生	16700
邱婷蔚	北一女中	16700
黃昱翔	建國中學	16700
游雅嵐	和平高中	16700
林敬富	師大附中	16700
曾乙晏	成功高中	16600
陳威任	南湖高中	16500
劉　瑄	松山高中	16500
余冠廷	建國中學	16500
范祐豪	師大附中	16500
郭致妤	基隆女中	16400
張宇揚	建國中學	16400
劉重均	北一女中	16400
劉祖亨	成淵高中	16400
許志遙	百齡高中	16400
周佑昱	建國中學	16300
蔡必婕	景美女中	16300
陳詩昀	北商學院	16200
范文棋	中崙高中	16200
何慧瑩	內湖高中	16200

姓名	學校	總金額
廖祥舜	永平高中	16200
黃白雲	成功高中	16100
吳雨宸	北一女中	16100
趙家德	衛理女中	16000
劉博馨	中和高中	15900
周柿均	北一女中	15900
賴冠儒	永春高中	15900
林俐妤	大直高中	15900
徐柏庭	延平國中部	15800
洪書婷	大同高中	15800
張博淵	延平高中	15800
鄭景文	師大附中	15800
吳杰穎	大同高中	15800
方仕翰	南山高中	15800
劉弘煒	師大附中	15800
王志嘉	建國中學	15800
廖子瑩	北一女中	15766
溫子漢	麗山高中	15750
許晉魁	政大附中	15750
吳庭語	景美女中	15700
林冠逸	中正高中	15700
林筱儒	中山女中	15700
秦知寧	中正高中	15600
張譽繻	成淵高中	15600
林裕騏	松山高中	15500
郭昌叡	建國中學	15500
翁鉦遠	格致高中	15500
何佩臻	永平高中	15400
王介竤	師大附中	15400
何思緯	內湖高中	15400
官鼎翔	大同高中	15300
吳姿穎	基隆高中	15300
張鈺婧	松山高中	15300
蔡昕叡	松山高中	15300
林于傑	師大附中	15300
蔡承翰	成功高中	15300
鄭竣陽	中和高中	15250
柯冠宇	中和高中	15200
游世群	建國中學	15100
李宜蒨	北一女中	14966
呂科進	成功高中	14900
林述君	松山高中	14850
翟恆威	師大附中	14850
魯怡佳	北一女中	14833
劉九榛	育成高中	14800
張爾蘭	中山女中	14800
林仕強	建國中學	14800
陳正和	師大附中	14800
林育正	師大附中	14800
周子芸	北一女中	14775
李念恩	建國中學	14750
盧彥錞	建國中學	14700

姓名	學校	總金額
顏意欣	北一女中	14700
張　安	建國中學	14700
黃姿瑋	中和高中	14700
蔡念臻	北一女中	14666
王奕婷	北一女中	14600
林勁延	成功高中	14600
黃柏榕	建國中學	14600
劉釋允	建國中學	14600
陳俐君	秀峰高中	14500
白哲睿	建國中學	14500
王惠姍	大同高中	14400
李禹逵	西松高中	14400
馬偉傑	成功高中	14400
廖珮函	北一女中	14375
賴韻如	華江高中	14300
黃柏綱	建國中學	14300
王亭雅	師大附中	14300
陳怡誠	建國中學	14300
洪懿亨	建國中學	14300
何昕叡	建國中學	14200
何昱葳	中山女中	14200
鍾承餘	成功高中	14200
吳御甄	中山女中	14200
蔡汶原	成功高中	14200
徐珮宜	板橋高中	14200
洪敏珊	景美女中	14200
顏士翔	政大附中	14200
張聿辰	建國中學	14100
蔣佳勳	中山女中	14100
陳柏誠	松山高中	14100
林冠宇	松山高中	14050
饒宇軒	政大附中	14000
張凱傑	建國中學	14000
楊祐瑋	中正高中	13900
朱宥臻	中山女中	13900
孫迦玫	金陵女中	13900
林政緯	成功高中	13900
蔡汶霖	大直高中	13850
陳　岳	建國中學	13800
黃乃芙	北一女中	13800
陳俊達	板橋高中	13800
陳胤竹	建國中學	13800
陳品文	建國中學	13800
劉子瑄	松山高中	13700
吳柏萱	建國中學	13700
魏廷龍	陽明高中	13700
施柏廷	板橋高中	13700
林學典	縣格致中學	13600
陳衍廷	東山高中	13600
易亞婷	景美女中	13600
張乃文	建國中學	13600
童　楷	師大附中	13600

姓名	學校	總金額
陳映彤	中山女中	13600
林雅晴	板橋高中	13600
戴章祐	成功高中	13500
林意紋	中和高中	13500
丘子軒	北一女中	13500
曾右濤	建國中學	13500
陳翔緯	建國中學	13500
劉聖廷	松山高中	13475
徐瑋澤	建國中學	13400
陳翊薇	北一女中	13400
楊明仁	建國中學	13400
張文馨	師大附中	13400
楊嘉祐	師大附中	13400
陳致元	建國中學	13400
周東林	百齡高中	13400
尤修鴻	松山高中	13300
莊庭秀	板橋高中	13300
張詩亭	北一女中	13300
黃乃婁	基隆女中	13300
周子鈞	師大附中	13300
林詠欣	北一女中	13200
陳裕文	板橋高中	13200
陳　皜	建國中學	13200
林子筠	中山女中	13200
卓漢庭	景美女中	13200
林芷伃	中山女中	13100
劉祐閩	成功高中	13100
林書佑	師大附中	13100
方　翔	成功高中	13100
韓月婄	中和高中	13100
林宜靜	明倫高中	13100
楊詠晴	國三重高中	13100
蔡安騏	師大附中	13100
陶俊成	成功高中	13100
李霖季	建國中學	13000
林宏杰	成功高中	13000
戴士傑	永春高中	13000
詹士賢	建國中學	13000
蕭傑尹	林口高中	13000
黃偉倫	成功高中	13000
徐浩芸	萬芳高中	13000
林奐妤	北一女中	12900
林鼎翔	建國中學	12900
曹　傑	松山高中	12850
雷力銘	東山高中	12700
吳佩勳	松山高中	12700
牛筱彣	景美女中	12700
施懿庭	師大附中	12700
李姿瑩	板橋高中	12700
廖宣懿	北一女中	12600
劉以增	板橋高中	12600
呂佳洋	成功高中	12600

www.learnschool.com.tw
劉毅英文教育機構
學費最低・效果最佳
高中部：台北市許昌街17號6F（捷運M8出口對面・學勤補習班） TEL：（02）2389-5212
國中部：台北市重慶南路一段10號7F（火車站前・學林補習班） TEL：（02）2361-6101
台中總部：台中市三民路三段125號7F（世界健身中心樓上） TEL：（04）2221-8861

心得筆記欄

中級英語寫作口說測驗

主　　　編 / 劉　毅

發 行 所 / 學習出版有限公司　　　☎ (02) 2704-5525

郵 撥 帳 號 / 0512727-2 學習出版社帳戶

登 記 證 / 局版台業 *2179* 號

印 刷 所 / 裕強彩色印刷有限公司

台 北 門 市 / 台北市許昌街 10 號 2 F　　☎ (02) 2331-4060

台灣總經銷 / 紅螞蟻圖書有限公司　　☎ (02) 2795-3656

美國總經銷 / Evergreen Book Store　☎ (818) 2813622

本公司網址　www.learnbook.com.tw

電 子 郵 件　learnbook@learnbook.com.tw

書＋MP3 一片售價：新台幣二百八十元正

2011 年 10 月 1 日新修訂

ISBN 978-957-519-998-2